Mary Earle Hardy

**The Hall of Shells**

Mary Earle Hardy

**The Hall of Shells**

ISBN/EAN: 9783337389574

Printed in Europe, USA, Canada, Australia, Japan

Cover: Foto ©Andreas Hilbeck / pixelio.de

More available books at **www.hansebooks.com**

# THE HALL OF SHELLS,

BY

## MRS. A. S. HARDY
AUTHOR OF THREE SINGERS

NEW YORK
D. APPLETON AND COMPANY
1897

# INTRODUCTION TO THE HOME READING BOOK SERIES BY THE EDITOR.

THE new education takes two important directions—one of these is toward original observation, requiring the pupil to test and verify what is taught him at school by his own experiments. The information that he learns from books or hears from his teacher's lips must be assimilated by incorporating it with his own experience.

The other direction pointed out by the new education is systematic home reading. It forms a part of school extension of all kinds. The so-called "University Extension" that originated at Cambridge and Oxford has as its chief feature the aid of home reading by lectures and round-table discussions, led or conducted by experts who also lay out the course of reading. The Chautauquan movement in this country prescribes a series of excellent books and furnishes for a goodly number of its readers annual courses of lectures. The teachers' reading circles that exist in many States prescribe the books to be read, and publish some analysis, commentary, or catechism to aid the members.

Home reading, it seems, furnishes the essential basis of this great movement to extend education

beyond the school and to make self-culture a habit
of life.

Looking more carefully at the difference between
the two directions of the new education we can see
what each accomplishes. There is first an effort to
train the original powers of the individual and make
him self-active, quick at observation, and free in his
thinking. Next, the new education endeavors, by the
reading of books and the study of the wisdom of the
race, to make the child or youth a participator in the
results of experience of all mankind.

These two movements may be made antagonistic
by poor teaching. The book knowledge, containing as
it does the precious lesson of human experience, may
be so taught as to bring with it only dead rules of
conduct, only dead scraps of information, and no
stimulant to original thinking. Its contents may be
memorized without being understood. On the other
hand, the self-activity of the child may be stimulated
at the expense of his social well-being—his originality
may be cultivated at the expense of his rationality.
If he is taught persistently to have his own way, to
trust only his own senses, to cling to his own opinions
heedless of the experience of his fellows, he is preparing for an unsuccessful, misanthropic career, and
is likely enough to end his life in a madhouse.

It is admitted that a too exclusive study of the
knowledge found in books, the knowledge which is
aggregated from the experience and thought of other
people, may result in loading the mind of the pupil
with material which he can not use to advantage.

Some minds are so full of lumber that there is no space left to set up a workshop. The necessity of uniting both of these directions of intellectual activity in the schools is therefore obvious, but we must not, in this place, fall into the error of supposing that it is the oral instruction in school and the personal influence of the teacher alone that excites the pupil to activity. Book instruction is not always dry and theoretical. The very persons who declaim against the book, and praise in such strong terms the self-activity of the pupil and original research, are mostly persons who have received their practical impulse from reading the writings of educational reformers. Very few persons have received an impulse from personal contact with inspiring teachers compared with the number that have received an impulse from such books as Herbert Spencer's Treatise on Education, Rousseau's Émile, Pestalozzi's Leonard and Gertrude, Francis W. Parker's Talks about Teaching, G. Stanley Hall's Pedagogical Seminary. Think in this connection, too, of the impulse to observation in natural science produced by such books as those of Hugh Miller, Faraday, Tyndall, Huxley, Agassiz, and Darwin.

The new scientific book is different from the old. The old style book of science gave dead results where the new one gives not only the results, but a minute account of the method employed in reaching those results. An insight into the method employed in discovery trains the reader into a naturalist, an historian, a sociologist. The books of the writers above named have done more to stimulate original research on the part of their readers than all other influences combined.

It is therefore much more a matter of importance to get the right kind of book than to get a living teacher. The book which teaches results, and at the same time gives in an intelligible manner the steps of discovery and the methods employed, is a book which will stimulate the student to repeat the experiments described and get beyond these into fields of original research himself. Every one remembers the published lectures of Faraday on chemistry, which exercised a wide influence in changing the style of books on natural science, causing them to deal with method more than results, and thus to train the reader's power of conducting original research. Robinson Crusoe for nearly two hundred years has stimulated adventure and prompted young men to resort to the border lands of civilization. A library of home reading should contain books that stimulate to self-activity and arouse the spirit of inquiry. The books should treat of methods of discovery and evolution. All nature is unified by the discovery of the law of evolution. Each and every being in the world is now explained by the process of development to which it belongs. Every fact now throws light on all the others by illustrating the process of growth in which each has its end and aim.

The Home Reading Books are to be classed as follows:

*First Division.* Natural history, including popular scientific treatises on plants and animals, and also descriptions of geographical localities. The branch of study in the district school course which corresponds to this is geography. Travels and sojourns in distant lands; special writings which treat of this or that animal or plant, or family of animals or plants; anything that relates to organic nature or to meteorology, or descriptive astronomy may be placed in this class.

*Second Division.* Whatever relates to physics or natural philosophy, to the statics or dynamics of air or water or light or electricity, or to the properties of matter; whatever relates to chemistry, either organic or inorganic—books on these subjects belong to the class that relates to what is inorganic. Even the so-called organic chemistry relates to the analysis of organic bodies into their inorganic compounds.

*Third Division.* History and biography and ethnology. Books relating to the lives of individuals, and especially to the social life of the nation, and to the collisions of nations in war, as well as to the aid that one gives to another through commerce in times of peace; books on ethnology relating to the manners and customs of savage or civilized peoples; books on the primitive manners and customs which belong to the earliest human beings—books on these subjects belong to the third class, relating particularly to the human will, not merely the individual will but the social will, the will of the tribe or nation; and to this third class belong also books on ethics and morals, and on forms of government and laws, and what is included under the term civics or the duties of citizenship.

*Fourth Division.* The fourth class of books includes more especially literature and works that make known the beautiful in such departments as sculpture, painting, architecture and music. Literature and art show human nature in the form of feelings, emotions, and aspirations, and they show how these feelings lead over to deeds and to clear thoughts. This department of books is perhaps more important than any other in our home reading, inasmuch as it teaches a knowledge of human nature and enables us to understand the motives that lead our fellow-men to action.

To each book is added an analysis in order to aid the reader in separating the essential points from the unessential, and give each its proper share of attention.

W. T. HARRIS.

Washington, D. C., *November 10, 1890.*

# PREFACE.

THE changing greens of the ocean, the wim-
ple of its waters when at peace, abide among
the pleasantest memories of my early childhood.
Glimpses into the sea, as pictured by Fouqué,
still have fascinations surpassing fact or fiction
of these later days.

This little book is published with the hope
that it may lead to a fuller study of some of
the most interesting and most beautiful creations in Nature. Books upon marine shells,
either not too expensive or too learned for common use, are few; hence it is hoped that this
little volume may help to awaken an interest
in the sea and its treasures, which can but grow
with the years and afford an ever-widening and
deepening source of delight and of profit.

Pearls let slip from their broken string, led
—in the story—to the hidden casket. So may

these simple studies be like bits of pearly wampum, leading to a thesaurus wherein is a treasure trove.

Mrs. A. S. Hardy.

Unionville, Ohio, *July, 1897.*

# CONTENTS.

| CHAPTER | | PAGE |
|---|---|---|
| I.—Four people and the hall of shells | | 3 |
| II.—The mermaid's tea service . . | | 13 |
| III.—Purpuras.—Murexes . . | | 27 |
| IV.—Microscopic shells . . | | 33 |
| V.—Ianthina.—Tritonia . | | 37 |
| VI.—Sea secrets . . . . . . . . | | 43 |
| VII.—A Portuguese man-of-war.—The Medusæ family . . . . . . . . . | | 51 |
| VIII.—Pearls.—Mother-of-pearl . . . . . | | 61 |
| IX.—Flowers of the sea.—Story of the mermaid's lace . . . . . . . . | | 73 |
| X.—The Argonaut.—The Nautilus . . . | | 83 |
| XI.—Rocked in the cradle of the deep . | | 93 |
| XII.—Gay, sad Scheveningen . . . | | 99 |
| XIII.—An ancient family . | | 109 |
| XIV.—Barnacles . . . . . | | 117 |
| XV.—A sea fan and a sea parable . . . . | | 123 |
| XVI.—A storm.—Razor fishes.—Byssus spinners.—Stone eaters.—Lighted tombs . . . . | | 135 |
| XVII.—Olives . . . . . | | 145 |
| XVIII.—Growth of shells . . . . | | 155 |
| XIX.—"Things unreck'd of " . . . . | | 163 |
| XX.—Trouble . . . . . . . . | | 169 |

xiii

# LIST OF FULL-PAGE ILLUSTRATIONS.

FACING
PAGE

Abalones . . . . . . . . *Frontispiece*

Listening to the smooth-lipped shell; Triton variegatus . 19

Pilgrim wearing his badge of knighthood . . 22

The legend of the Tyrian dye . . . . 28

The comb of pearl . . . . . . . . 29

"One-seated shallops whose boatmen have departed" . 51

Hydroids and jelly-fish . . . . . . 56

Pearl-producing shells 64

The mermaid's lace . 78

The argonaut . . . . . . . 84

Scheveningen shell-gatherer . . . . . . 106

A sea lily . . . . . . . . . . 111

Fishing for sea cucumbers in the Philippine Islands; Holothuridæ . . . . . . . . . 113

Barnacles . . . . . . . . . 119

A fan gorgon; Hermit crab . . . . . . . 131

Ianthina communis, or violet snail, with float supporting
eggs; Patella vulgata; Empty shell of Ianthina; Ensis
ensis, or razor shell . . . . . . . . 139

Conus textile; Conus imperialis; Oliva scripta; Oliva por-
phyrea; Phasianella ventricosa; Murex princeps . . 151

# ANALYSIS OF HALL OF SHELLS,

## *WITH SUGGESTIONS FOR FURTHER STUDY.*

THE following paragraphs are intended more as helps to those who may wish to continue studies here begun than as any perfect analysis of chapters. The books which have been especially helpful in preparing these studies are here indicated, and their helpfulness acknowledged.

As will be seen, authorities are sometimes referred to and studies suggested which do not relate to shells at all, but from the nature of this little volume have seemed to belong here.

CHAPTER I.—Introduction of our friends the Bremelys to the new minister, and the ocean whose name is Peace. Interest in the starfish and the *Haliotis* begun ; the mouth and stomach of the former indicated, and the nervous system of the latter. For further understanding of these consult zoölogies and encyclopædias. For runes of the Northmen read the Sagas, Scandinavian mythology, and Odin, by Carlyle. The works of Fouqué, whom Richter christened "The Valiant," furnish weird and graceful tales of the sea. Read the classics, in original or translations.

CHAPTER II.—The *Pecten* and *Patella* have been used as plates and drinking vessels at different times and by various nations ; the former served as a badge of knighthood. The beauty and wonderful construction of the

2                                     xvii

mollusks tenanting these shells surpass the marvelously
contrived houses in which they live. The power of adhesion possessed by the *Patella* and its ability to sustain
great weights should be tested by those who have access
to seacoasts. Read Mollusca, their Shells, Tongues, Eyes,
and Ears, by Philip Henry Gosse, F. R. S. Examine common garden snails, comparing their eyes with those of the
*Pecten* upon the seacoast.

CHAPTER III.—The extensive use of *Purpuras* and
*Murexes* in the ancient dying of purples is shown by the
little mountains of shells still lying in vicinities where
this industry was plied. The coloring matter—but a drop
—contained in a veinlike sac. The *Purpura* the crest of
the city of Tyre. Study Tyre, and learn of the caldron-
like cavities in the rocks where these shells were crushed.
Compare the shells of this family, noting how the whorls
of some of these shells are thickened by varices or nodes,
indicating rest periods in growth; also the immense development of the last whirl in some; the elongated spines
in others.

CHAPTER IV.—Observe with a strong microscope the
beauty of coil and polish in the most minute shells.
Where living specimens can be examined the tenants of
these diminutive shells will be found to possess as complicated and delicate organisms as those of larger growth.
Study sand from any sea beach. Shake the sand and
atoms from sponges on sale, then count and examine the
treasures you will find.

CHAPTER V.—Undine finds a "sea horn" among her
shells. It is the shell Neptune's trumpeter is fabled to
have used to still the tumult of the sea. *Tritonia tritonis*
used as a teakettle, the operculum its cover. *Ianthina fragilis,* preserved through the beating of waves and the
grinding of sand, bears its egg capsules beneath a float,
and buoyed up upon the tossing seas the delicate creatures
are born to the purple.

The horny operculum of land snails may be seen, and

its connection by strong muscle with the animal tested. Look up in an encyclopædia how the cartilaginous air vesicles composing the egg float of the sea snail are secreted and how attached.

CHAPTER VI.—The dip net brings up marvels undreamed of before ; the brine and mud become full of lessons; hydroids, scalaria, stomapod, and *Sapphirina* give up their secrets. The sea bottom is shown by science to be more than a fairyland. A dip net may be used in study in either salt or fresh water. Read The Bottom of the Sea, by T. Sourel.

CHAPTER VII.—The *Physalia* or Portuguese man-of-war is sometimes driven up from the tropic seas and stranded. It is one of the most interesting of the *Medusæ* family; armed with poison-filled tentacles which are its weapons of defense, and by them its food is obtained. The study of the *Medusæ*, either in books or actual life, watching development, will fill many days with delightful employment. In fresh water, common Hydra may be found under leaves of aquatic plants. Cut them in pieces and see their power of reproduction from the severed pieces. Turn them inside out and see the result.

CHAPTER VIII.—Origin of pearls was formerly accounted for by drops of dew becoming solidified. Pearls are formed over hard, offensive matter within the folds of the mantle, also secreted and used as nacre by the animal in mending points of irritation. Pearls most highly esteemed by all nations and at all times. Pearls are of various colors and each color has its peculiar votaries. The pearl Cleopatra drank questioned by science.

The rainbow shells of the *Haliotidæ* called *Awabi* in Japan, abalone in California. The iridescence of their nacreous lining due to the laminations of nacre secreted by the animal and irregularly overlapping in delicate films. Read Precious Stones, by Harry Emanuel.

CHAPTER IX.—Term *Algæ* now includes much less than formerly, many specimens once held as vegetable now consigned to animal kingdom. Have been variously classified, and the old classifications abandoned or giving place to those relating more particularly to structure and development.

*Algæ* draw their sustenance from the water, loving best the quiet seas of temperate zones, and depending upon light for their coloring. Find authority for the story in studies upon the ancient art of Venetian point lace.

To secure and preserve the most delicate varieties of seaweed, slip a paper under them while floating in the sea or a dish of water, raise carefully, arranging any imperfect points with fine camel's-hair brush or the point of a pin. Kelp must be pressed between oiled paper or pieces of muslin on account of the glue it contains. A gatherer of seaweeds when questioned regarding many varieties replied, "Oh, nobody knows!" Here, then, is a realm waiting and luring investigation.

CHAPTER X.—Argonaut and nautilus—both cephalopods—are quite unlike in many points, yet their names have been indiscriminately used. There is a similarity in the form of their shells; that of the argonaut is, however, thin and [brittle, while the shell of the nautilus is thick and strong. This latter is divided into chambers, hence called the chambered nautilus. It is interesting to study the fossil species of these shells.

CHAPTER XI.—The family *Veneridæ* contains many beauties long ago dedicated to Venus. Varieties of these shells are numerous, but all more or less beautifully sculptured and pictured. The value the aborigines attached to the round clam of the Atlantic coast has been preserved in its name *Venus mercenaria*. Clams may be studied in salt and fresh waters, the number and character of the teeth in their hinges observed. "The nervous system can be, with care and patience, worked out in the clam or fresh water mussel."

The family *Chitonidæ* are curiously constructed, enabling the animal to accommodate itself to rounded sur-faces. Its shell consists of eight pieces.

CHAPTER XII.—Scheveningen, Holland's famous and fashionable resort, has its two villages and its two lives. The character of its people seems invigorated by their hard-ships. Its sand dunes, its sand beach, and its novel bath-ing arrangements are well given in Holland and its Peo-ple, by De Amicis.

CHAPTER XIII.—The *Echidermata* is a spiny family as well as a family of distinction and beauty, all adhering more or less closely to the example and characteristics of their ancient ancestry. If possible, study living starfish, the fossils of this family, and compare the plan of the leath-ery exterior of *Holothurians* with the delicate plates of the *Echinus miliaris*, and examine the spines of the latter and their wonderful adjustment.

CHAPTER XIV.—In external appearance barnacles re-semble mollusks, in organism they are crustaceans. The changes accomplished in their various stages are explained in works upon zoölogy.

CHAPTER XV.—The *Gordonidœ*, which were long be-lieved to be singular and gorgeous sea plants, are now known as the home and work of polypi. Some grow in long branch-like extensions, others look like network of jewels. Their relatives are the polypi—creators of the corals. The soft bodies of these builders are uniform in structure and close-ly adhere to their enlarged type—the sea anemone. Ex-amine and compare structure of different corals.

CHAPTER XVI.—Storms destroy many shells while oth-ers equally fragile are lifted to places of safety upon the crest of the waves. Some burrow in the sand, as the *Si-phonida*, and are discovered by the jets of water they spout out when disturbed. Others are moored by cables of their own spinning : these are the byssus spinners, and notches may be observed in shells of this kind allowing of the passage of the byssus, which the animal attaches at will. Borers also excavate retreats in wood or rock, even sometimes completely burying themselves in sepulchers of their own making. See the work of pholades in the columns of the ancient temple of Serapis, at Pozzuolis.

CHAPTER XVII.—Among the most beautiful of shells are those of *Oliridæ*. The markings of some suggest delicate cuneiform and picture writing. The external surface of these is pictured entirely different from the decorations on layers just below. These mollusks have the ability to dissolve away earlier formed volutions. Study olives and cone shells in Structural and Systematic Conchology, by George W. Tryon.

CHAPTER XVIII.—Shells were once parts of the mantle or delicate films secreted by and thrown off from it; there harden, and unite with other tissues previously thrown off. Observe these layers joined to each other as shown in the more solid shell—the *Cassides*, for example.

The color of shells also the secreting work of the mantle; tints dependent upon light. Still, how is a mystery. Observe under valves of shells where light has not reached.

CHAPTER XIX.—See Land Shells, published by American Tract Society, for lessons upon the eyes of snails, and apparent affection among them. Sounds are produced by some varieties of sea slugs. Auditorial nerves are discovered in some shellfishes. Their whole surface extremely sensitive.

CHAPTER XX.—In the family *Cypræidæ* we find the beautiful porcelain shells which change their exquisite markings with different stages of growth. In this family members of the genus *Ovulum* are beautifully enameled, but lack the coloring of the *Cypræa*.

# FOUR PEOPLE
## AND THE HALL OF SHELLS.

O ever-solitary sea,
  Of which we all have found
Somewhat to dream or say—the type
  Of things without a bound—
Love, long as life, and strong as death;
  Faith, humble as sublime;
Eternity, whose large depths hold
  The wrecks of this small Time.
MISS MULOCK.

And Nature, the old nurse, took
  The child upon her knee,
Saying, "Here is a story book
  Thy Father has written for thee."
LONGFELLOW.

2

## FOUR PEOPLE AND THE HALL OF SHELLS.

"OLD Neptune's napping!" said Tom, as he watched the waves that played as lightly as a baby's fingers with the sands upon the shore.

Far out, the sea was blue as bluest amethyst; slowly circling toward the land the waves grew green and opaline; their jewels flashed a moment in the sun and were drawn back again into the sea.

Miss Bremely, to whom Tom had spoken, seemed under the same spell as the ocean; her eyes held in their blue depths a dreamy look of peace; the sunshine touched her hair to gold, gave a glint of richness to brow and cheek, and fell in light caress upon her folded hands.

She answered Tom with a smile, then rousing from her reverie, she said, "Our ocean is for the nonce living up to Magellan's good opinions and to the name the old navigator gave it so long ago."

Almost before her sentence was finished, Tom, who spied a stranger working a dip net down the beach, with true boyish instinct had sped away to the scene of interest.

Still Miss Bremely mused in the hazy sunshine, the water lapping lightly against the rock upon which she sat. Bending over its ledge she gathered tangles of sea kelp the waves laid at her feet.

"Thank you, dear old Sea," she said; "you are gentle and sing like a siren to-day; to-morrow you may roar like an army of Titans. Ah, well, your calms and silvery tides are all the dearer to us because of your depths we can not fathom, your storms we can not quell."

Kneeling upon the sand she bent her head until the incoming waves touched her forehead with their crystal chrism, then rising she took her hamper of shells and started along an ascending pathway to a cottage not far distant among acacia trees. The cottage was her home. Turning from its main entrance she chose a winding flight of steps leading to a small balcony. There she paused before an open door and a childish voice greeted her with, "O Cousin Ellen, you look like a mermaid!"

Miss Bremely's hands were filled with treasures from the beach and her cheeks flushed to the delicate tint of sea shells, while the kelp she had wound about her hat, trailing down, had caught in the loose wefts of her hair and fell in tangles of color over the gray folds of her gown. But far better than the charm of a mermaid was the gentle grace of a loving spirit which brought sunshine into the room and joy to the child face that lay among the pillows.

Following Miss Bremely came Tom. Tom was preciously human. There was no hint of mermen about him. His trousers were rolled to the knees and gave evidence of having been touched by the waves. He carried his hat piled with limpets, spirals, and shining abalones, while his many bulging pockets suggested scores of hidden treasures.

Undine, the child among the pillows, was Tom's little sister,—though Undine was not her name at all. She was christened Gertrude. It had been her mother's name, and seemed to belong to the little girl whose cheerful spirit and gentle grace made her so like the sweet mother who had been borne away over the mystical seas by the same bark that brought the little girl to earth. Her father's niece, Miss Bremely, was as mother and companion to the child, and, seeing her love for the sea, it was she who had called her Undine ; and Undine she had become to every one saving her father. To him she was always Gertrude, and the name fell from his lips with a caressing tenderness as if he spoke to the sweet mother in heaven as well as to the child upon earth.

Tom's little sister was as frail as he was sturdy, and to alleviate the child's weariness when constrained to lie for months among her pillows, Miss Bremely wove her tales of the sea. At one time it was a rune of the Northmen, terrible with dragon ships, jötuns, and stormy seas, but beautiful with love and valor. At another it was a bit of classic lore made so simple and charming that Undine forgot her pain and longed for the time when she could read such wonderful stories herself. But even more fascinating than these were the descriptions of coral groves through which the Undine of Fouqué's charming stories walked, and the gardens, fathoms down, where gay-tinted flowers of the sea unfolded their delicate frondlike branches, independent alike of sunshine and shower.

She had wondered why such gardens grew far from any mortal sight, and Miss Bremely answered:

"There may be eyes that read these gospels
Other than the eyes of men."

When the child was busy, one day, sorting her shells, Miss Bremely told her of Ossian's lordly cave with its "hall of shells where kings and warriors feasted," and Undine had asked that, because of her love for the sea and because her name was that of a sea maiden, her room might be a hall of shells. Her cousin consented upon the conditions that Undine learn the names and what she could of the haunts and habits of her treasures. So Undine's room, opening toward the ocean, became a little hall of shells, and those who loved her brought their treasures into it, until it was growing to look like an ocean cave or a mermaid's throne room.

It was here that Miss Bremely and Tom came after their walk upon the strand. Miss Bremely placed her basket of shells upon a table by the bed, while Tom, with more devotion than discretion, dumped his dripping treasures upon the coverlet before his sister.

Miss Bremely's smothered "O Tom!" was unheard as Tom, with hands deep in his bulging pockets, exclaimed:

"Old Pacific must have been thinking about you, Undine; our cove was full of

shells. Guess I've found you some new ac-
quaintances. Just look at that beauty—pink
as a flower! The new minister was down on
the beach. He said *that* shell was a great trav-
eler and had come from the tropic seas.

"Undine, that minister knew me! Said he
saw me at church. I didn't s'pose ministers
ever saw boys. Our other minister never did.
I wouldn't wonder if Dr. McLean—that's the
new minister's name—knew 'most as much as
Cousin Ellen does about the ocean and its inhabitants. He showed me where to look to
find the mouth and stomach of a starfish; they
are right handy together, I tell you! He says
starfish are very fond of oysters. You wouldn't
s'pose they could open an oyster shell, would
you? But they can; they just put that queer
mouth of theirs close to the closed edge of the
oyster shell and inject a bitter liquid into the
shell; Mr. Oyster don't like the dose and opens
his valves, in walks the starfish and eats 'oyster on the half shell' without as much as a
thank you! Dr. McLean says these starfish
have a cousin that grows on a long stem like a
flower.

"See all these rainbow colors," he continued, displaying a brilliant *Haliotis*. "Dr.
McLean says the animal that lived in this shell

had a heart and a digestive and nervous system. He told me what these little 'portholes'
along the top are for, and showed me where to
look to find a limpet's eyes.

"I never knew before that ministers cared
about shells. I didn't s'pose they could talk
about much, 'cept 'Gyptians, Hebrews, and original sin!"

After a moment's pause, he added con-
vincingly, "Dr. McLean's very interesting for a
minister."

By this time Tom's pockets were emptied,
and Undine's eyes sparkling over her treasures;
the strands of kelp, too, were untangled from
Miss Bremely's hat and hair. They proved
to be very fine specimens, and were placed in
a press to dry, with strips of muslin on either
side to prevent their adhering to the paper of
the press.

# THE MERMAID'S TEA SERVICE.

3

Shells are at once the attraction of the untutored savage, the delight of the refined artist, the wonder of the philosophic zoölogist, and most valued treasure of the geologist. They adorn the sands of the sea-girt isles and continents now; and they form the earliest "footprints on the sands of time" in the history of our globe.—CARPENTER.

                              . . . I have seen
A curious child applying to her ear
The convolutions of a smooth-lipped shell,
To which, in silence hushed, her very soul
Listened intently and her countenance soon
Brightened with joy; for murmuring from within
Were heard sonorous cadences, whereby,
To her belief, the monitor expressed
Mysterious union with its native sea.
                              WORDSWORTH.

## II.

### THE MERMAID'S TEA SERVICE.

NATURE reveals most wonderful secrets to those who love her. Undine, bending over her treasures with glowing face, uttered many an exclamation of surprise and delight as she discovered new friends, or had charming secrets revealed to her from the lips of old.

She amused herself by arranging upon her tray a score or more of shells, delicately tinted, fair and shining as the rarest china, and not very dissimilar in shape to many of the dainty dishes of the day.

" Come, Cousin Ellen," she exclaimed, " and see my mermaid's tea service ! "

" Others than the Nereids have eaten and drank from beautiful vessels like these," said her cousin. "'This," she continued taking a shell from the tray, " is a *Pecten*, or scallop. One variety of *Pecten* served as a drinking cup in early times, and when the ancient chief-tain, Ossian, with his lordly guests, ' struck his sounding shells,' and when in his hall the 'shell of kings was heard,' it was probably such scallop cups the warriors clashed.

"Another *Pecten* was called the pilgrim's shell, and was used by the early Crusaders as both plate and goblet. This shell was sometimes from four to five inches broad, and found in abundance on the coast of Palestine. It was also worn upon the front of the hat as a badge of knighthood by those who had performed the sacred pilgrimages or visited a shrine of St. James. This latter gave it the additional name of St. James's shell, its proper name being *Pecten Jacobæus*.

"The name *Pecten* means comb, and has been given these shells because of the appearance of ribs ornamenting the surface of many varieties.

"But beautiful as are these shells, the mollusks living in such houses as these are even more beautiful and instructive.

"By quick opening and shutting of its valves the little animal moves through the water. When 'at home' the pretty creature lies upon one side, its two valves open far enough to admit of our peering in; there we see delicate white fringes waving this way and that, withdrawn and again floating over the edge of the shell. These are called tentacles, and among them can be discerned tiny and brilliant points which are shown by the lens to shine like diamonds, each rimmed in a setting of red. These are the eyes of the scallop, and Divine thought has protected them by the over-hanging shell rim as kindly and carefully as human eyes are shielded.

"We sometimes find the bright yellow eggs of this little animal, looking not unlike the roe of some fishes, but carefully deposited among the ruffles of the interior.

"The dainty dishes of your tea service are not all *Pectens*, however; here are limpets tinted and polished above the most famous china. *Patellæ*, or limpets, are found in many varie-ties ; one upon the western coast of South Amer-ica is a foot in diameter, and often serves as a dish. Indeed the name *Patella* signifies a dish.

"One is called the 'cup-and-saucer limpet' because of the cuplike formation in the inte-rior of the saucerlike shell. Another here upon your tray is called the 'keyhole limpet' on account of the tiny aperture you see in the apex of the shell.

"Shells of this family have long been used as ornaments as well as dishes. Necklaces

have been strung of them, and such are found
in some of the most ancient sepulchers.

"When you are well enough to go down
to the beach you will wonder at the power
of adhesion possessed by these little limpets,
for it is impossible to remove them from the
rocks without breaking their shells unless they
are surprised by sudden seizure.

"Some authorities say this is owing to the
large round foot of the *Patella*, which is very
muscular and possessed of a viscous secretion
which aids it as a sucker. The perfectly even
edge of the shell keeps it tight against the
rock, while 'the power of treating a vacuum'
—a problem too old for your young head—
is said also to enter into the operation.
Others attribute the adhesion to no muscular
action, but chiefly to the 'invisible glue which
exudes from the granulated base of the sole of
its foot,' as the expansion upon which the animal moves is called. We find upon removing
one of these little creatures from the rocks
that a sticky secretion is left where the limpet
clung. This gluelike substance is soon dissolved by the action of the sea water.

"A weight of from twenty-eight to thirty
pounds has been suspended from the shell of a
limpet attached to a stone; the weight was

sustained by the plucky little animal for some seconds. Whatever theory may be correct in accounting for the strength with which these little creatures cling to their rocky home, we can wholly agree with Wordsworth who wrote:

> "Should the strongest arm endeavor
>     The limpet from its rock to sever,
> 'Tis seen its loved support to clasp
>     With such tenacity of grasp,
> We wonder that such strength should dwell
>     In such a small and simple shell!

"When the water covers his weather-worn dome, the limpet does a-walking go; but always returns to the same spot upon the rock and remains fixed while the tides are out, as its gills were never made for breathing air. When the rocks are soft, the little limpet wears away not only his 'door stone,' but its circular little dome reposes in a cavity which its muscular foot scoops out, and which the shell exactly fits.

"Who would guess this silent little creature possessor of a tongue twice as long as its shell? Stranger still, this ribbonlike tongue is furnished with rows of teeth. The *Patella vulgaris* of the British Isles has one hundred and sixty rows of teeth upon its tongue, and twelve teeth in a row, making its entire 'set' to consist of

nineteen hundred and twenty teeth. When
not in use mowing the rocks which are coated
with seaweed, the tongue with its rows of shining teeth is comfortably coiled away in its mysterious and wonderfully contrived interior."

" I never guessed my mermaid's dishes held
such a feast of wisdom," laughed Undine.

" Your pretty shells are finer than the rarest
china, and suggest others that have been similarly used in the early days of our country.

" There are two varieties of pear conch upon
the Atlantic coast—the *Fulgur carica* and the
*Fulgur canaliculatus*—which the aborigines
used as drinking vessels. From the pearly surfaces of these shells their white wampum was
cut, which was the shell money as well as
charmed ornament of the Indians ; knives were
also cut from these shells."

Through the open door Undine caught
glimpses of the sea and exclaimed :

" Dear old Ocean, how I love you ! What
treasures you send me ! And, Cousin Ellen,
you are my good genie who charm away my
pains; the stories you tell me are better than
fairy tales and make me forget that I am not
strong.  I seem, like the old German's Undine,
to wander away with the ocean sprites and to
know their mysterious and happy life.  The

LISTENING TO THE SMOOTH-LIPPED SHELL.
TRITON VARIEGATUS.

sea shouts and laughs and beckons to me, even my shells are full of sea songs;" and she held a chambered shell to her ear, talking of its plaintive murmur, so like the breaking of waves upon a far-off coast.

A few minutes later she was asleep, the shell still held to her ear, and a smile upon her lips—a sign of the pleasantness of her voyage over sleep's mysterious sea.

This is what she saw: A quaint little creature came up out of the waves and stood upon the sand. It looked like a bit of a crumpled veil, a weird little wraith made up of frills and ruffles, but with a foot so large as to suggest a mistake had been made in the adjustment.

Undine, with her love for all manner of sea tenants, smiled a welcome, then waited curiously, uncertain what might be the next propriety in view of her guest being incognito. Presently a voice, finer than the vibration of a spider's silken string, came to Undine between the noise of the waves, and the little visitor announced:

"*I* built that pearly palace you are holding in your hand; *I* painted its walls and tinted the ceiling of its chambers. It was my home for years, how many you can tell by counting the

thickened varices upon its surface, each of
which marks a year of my life and the season
of rest that came to me after my toils. I pride
myself no one could have fashioned a fairer
dwelling, and when at length I was torn from
it I left its halls filled with memories. Those
smallest coils echo with the songs of life's
morning; its joys as well as its sorrows are all
repeated there. Upon one side you may see a
pearly scar. It was there that a borer pierced
my walls while the shell was yet tender. The
thrills of horror of that moment still haunt
those small chambers. Rescue came and I
lived to mend the broken wall, but you will
see the scar remains.

"Later the walls of my citadel were again
pierced and the horrible borer once more
sought my life; but again I was delivered.
This time I had grown too large for these
small chambers, and if you will carefully examine the interior of my house you will see a
partition is built shutting off the broken and
outgrown chambers. Those are painful memories, and mingled with the merrier music in the
coils you may hear cries that are wild and
plaintive.

"Upon the island sands where I was cast I
once heard a wise man say, 'Sorrow gives some

of the sweetest strains to life's music.' I do not know. You may listen and learn for yourself.

"The next room is filled with the singing of sirens and laughter of sea nymphs as they leap from crag to crag under the sea. If you listen well you may catch, too, the sigh of a sailor boy as he fell asleep.

"The outer whirls and the vestibule retain the pleasant murmur of winds through palms and spice trees of a sea-girt island, the pleasant lapping of waves upon the sand, and the laughter of bathers in the surf. Through all and above all is heard the ceaseless roar of the ocean.

"I can not explain to you the mysterious union between myself and my native sea, whereby sighs and sobbings as from a heart oppressed become forever my heritage.

"But the gray old sea has a secret, a mysterious and terrible sorrow. By the thought of it he is transformed, and white with rage he breaks rocks to atoms and tears continents in his fury. Again he falls to sobbing so piteously that we all sob with him. The secret of his sorrow is a long, sad tale; but I will tell it to you, and why he moans and raves, why he sobs and sighs. Listen!"

At this up sped a white wave from the sea. It caught the little ruffled and frilled wraith of the shell, and with a single sweep drew her into its darkest depths, out of sight forever.

A limpet, *Patella vulgata*, with its dome-like house, is shown in our engraving, in which are also the sea snails and the razor-shell.

The illustration of the Palmer or Pilgrim shows the manner in which scallop shells were worn as badges of a holy knighthood. An empty St. James's shell—*Pecten Jacobæus*—lies in the left foreground of the picture, while in the right is a shell with its living inmate, displaying the delicate fringelike tentacles as seen playing lightly in the water when the valves of the shell are slightly opened.

Between these lies a *Fusus* or spindle shell, well named—long, slender, thin-lipped, and without varices.

Upon each side are arranged several species of *Serpula*, which look like little stone serpents with their plumed and crimson crests. Annelids they are, their shelly, twisted tubes twining round and fastening themselves upon shells, stones, and other submarine objects, sometimes completely covering them. The dwellers in these calcareous, contorted tubes

PILGRIM WEARING HIS BADGE OF KNIGHTHOOD.

are themselves gay with color; indeed, the sea
folk in general delight in rich and delicate hues,
if we may judge from their beautifully painted
bodies and dwellings.

The tubelike homes which these gay sea
worms inhabit, are of their own construction
from lime and cement which their bodies secrete, and each is furnished with a curious
door which the owner of the fortress is able to
close upon the slightest alarm with lightning
rapidity.

The different varieties of *Serpula* are interesting and attractive embellishments to our
aquariums, and the marvelous arrangement of
delicate membranes and muscular fibers of
these extremely sensitive organisms well repay
our study.

# PURPURAS.—MUREXES.

The beggar wears thy purple as his own.

Miss Mulock.

Who would be
A mermaid fair,
Singing alone,
Combing her hair
Under the sea,
In a golden curl
With a comb of pearl ?

Tennyson.

26

III.

PURPURAS.—MUREXES.

LOOKING over the shells upon the table, Miss Bremely found a pretty tuberculated shell of the *Muricidæ* family. She told Undine its name—*Purpura emarginata.*

"It has a pretty relative," said Miss Bremely, "which is used by the South Sea Islanders as a drinking cup, and both belong to that famous family which yielded the royal purple dye anciently so highly prized by those who wore 'soft raiment' and dwelt in 'kings' houses.'

"The dye was a colorless fluid which became purple upon exposure to the sun; it was but a drop, and secreted in a veinlike sac near the head of the little *Murex.* No wonder that purple stuffs were costly, being valued, we are told, as high as two hundred dollars a pound.

"To-day, beside the ruined city which gave its name to these purples, lie other ruins—piles

4                          27

of shattered homes of the *Murex trunculus* or Tyrian rock shell.

"The centuries have preserved a pretty story celebrating the origin of this industry— the coloring of purple. It has an idyllic charm, and brings the people of that old city, whose crest was a *Purpura* shell, near enough to be our kin. A pretty Tyrian maiden, so runs the tale, was tripping along the sea sands ; her pet was a dog that sported at her side ; in his play he took a shell in his mouth and crushed it ; soon the dog's white hair was dashed with the richest purple. The pretty maiden had a lover whom no undertaking daunted ; she showed to him the beautiful color upon the hair of her pet, and begged that she might have a robe of the same rich hue. Not many days thereafter the hero-lover brought the pretty maiden the first robe of royal purple ever worn.

"Other members of this family have also furnished the purple dye. At one place in southern Greece there is a little 'mountain of shells' of the *Murex brandaris,* crushed for their purple. Several of the *Purpuras* were similarly used. Both *Murices* and *Purpuras* feed upon mollusks, boring through their shells with their hard-toothed proboscis. They are a numerous family, and at home in all seas,

THE LEGEND OF THE TYRIAN DYE.

THE COMB OF PEARL.

though the largest and most beautiful are found in the tropics.

"The regularly arranged spines upon many of the shells of this family give them a curious and to some varieties a very beautiful appearance. The 'black murex' (*Murex radix*), with its decorations like fringes of brown and black, comes from the tropics, and is a beautiful shell. Its rival, however, is the 'rose murex' (*Murex palma-rosæ*) from Ceylon, bordered with richest brown and lined with delicate rose.

"The 'woodcock shell' (*Murex tennispina*) is a singular, spiny variety of *Murex*, with a long and slender beak. It is called Venus's comb. This and the following one are the shells the poets call the 'comb of pearl,' and sing of how with it the mermaid

> "Sits on diamond rocks,
> Sleeking her soft, alluring locks.

*Murex tribulus*, found in the Indian seas, has a pearly shell with very thin, regular, and elongated spines."

Where the mermaid is seen in our picture combing her hair with her comb of pearl, the beautiful *Murex tennispina* is the "comb"; and the large number of long, parallel curved spines and the recurved shorter ones with

which it is adorned are plainly seen at the
bottom of that page, where is the larger illustration of the same shell.

The *Murex princeps* is the spiny shell
shown among the olive and cone shells.  It is
a beautiful variety, found upon the west coast
of South America, is sometimes five inches in
length. ˙ Its ribs are white, contrasting beautifully with its spines and shadings of chestnut
brown.

The *Muricidæ*, however, are not all regarded
as lovely.  It is a *Murex* which is one of the
worst enemies of the oyster, piercing its shell
and sucking the sweet juices from within.  So
voracious is this depredator that a large number of the bivalves are often required to furnish it a single meal, the young *Murex* select-
ing the young oyster shells, which are most
easily pierced, while the old *Murex* feasts upon
the large oysters, finding the labor of boring
through their hard shells but whets its appe-
tite for more.  The oyster farms in some parts
of Europe are only preserved by fishers being
employed incessantly to destroy these depre-
dators.                                ·

# MICROSCOPIC SHELLS.

Nothing imperfect or deficient left
Of all that He created.

MILTON.

Earth's crammed with heaven,
And every common bush afire with God;
But only he who sees takes off his shoes.

MRS. BROWNING.

## MICROSCOPIC SHELLS.

The sand among the shells was brushed into a tray, and with a microscope Undine found it contained tiny shells with colors and coils equaling even the large spirals and iridescent abalones which had so taken Tom's fancy.

Miss Bremely told her that in a pound of sand taken from the Adriatic, by computation two hundred thousand individuals were found; many more must have suffered wreck from the rough tossing and rubbing of the waves and sand. In an ounce of sand from Cape May it was estimated over thirty-five thousand individuals of a single species were discovered.

She was told that the sands of some beaches are composed almost entirely of shells, variously and perfectly formed, while the complicated organisms and harmonious contrivances of the animals inhabiting them must fill the beholder with amazement.

Undine sat for a long time picking one

speck after another out of the sand, her aston-
ishment and delight ever increasing as she
found such tiny spirals beautifully polished or
· clear as glass, with every coil perfect. Baby
bivalves were there with carvings so delicate
only a strong glass could trace them. From
some of the shells finest of threadlike feelers
protruded, showing such living atoms as perfect and as wonderful as are the houses they
inhabit.

"O Cousin Ellen!" she exclaimed, as the
revelation overwhelmed her, "how precious our
world must be to God! He has crowded even
its unseen places with such beauty and made
so perfect, things no human eye can see!"

"His wonderful works teach of him without whom 'was not anything made that was
made,'" replied her cousin. "In them he
gives us glimpses of his character. In his
creations, 'never more great than when mi-
nutely great,' he shows us his love for what is
perfect—the beautiful we call it. He keeps
these examples everywhere before us, as if he
would lure us to love what is perfect and to
become such ourselves."

# IANTHINA.—TRITONIA.

Walled by ranks of steadfast giants,
Fringed by leagues of shining sea.

*Anon.*

Have sight of Proteus rising from the sea,
Or hear old Triton blow his wreathèd horn.

WORDSWORTH.

36

## IANTHINA.—TRITONIA.

In another land—beloved of the Bremelys
—it was winter. In their California home the
petals of flowers fell light as snowflakes, and
the roaring of the ocean was to them in place
of the tumult of the north wind.

To the east of them blue mountains en-
camped, with their feet among flowers and their
broad shoulders to the siroccos that swept over
the plain.

Mr. Bremely hoped in this valley of flowers,
roses might flush his little daughter's cheeks,
where through all the ten years of her life
only lilies had bloomed.

At the close of his busy days her room
was the sacred spot to which he hastened, and
while he bent over her couch or her golden
head rested upon his shoulder, he looked with
a longing that was pain, for signs of coming
strength which physicians had prophesied
might follow this sojourn by the sea.

Every evening the child rejoiced in receiving some simple token of the love that had filled his thoughts all day. Sometimes it was fruit grown mellow and sweet in California's amber sun, or a cluster of roses fragrant as love.

This evening of which we write a box of shells was before her, and her father rejoiced in seeing her eyes sparkle as the eyes of happy children who are well.

She took a long, pointed shell from the box, exclaiming, "Cousin Ellen, papa has brought me a sea horn to call my mermaids to their banquet!" And placing the shell to her lips she blew mimic rounds upon her horn until a flush came into her cheeks, and seeing it her father's eyes were dim for joy.

"You pretty purple thing," she said, as she selected another shell from the collection her father had brought her, "are you a shell at all, I wonder, or are you a sea violet?"

The greater part of the shell that she held in her hand was purple as the veins in her wrist, but to add to its delicate beauty the spire was shaded to white.

"*Ianthina fragilis* is its name, or the 'sea snail' it is sometimes called," said her Cousin Ellen. "It is one of the daintiest and most fragile things that sails the seas. Its thin, pellucid, gossamerlike shell can not bear the rough handling of the waves. The snail that lives in this amethystine house swims by means of an air float secreted by and attached to its foot. To the under side of this float the egg capsules are securely fastened, and here the baby *Ianthina* is 'born to the purple.'

"Your trumpet shell is a *Tritonia*, and instead of sounding for a banquet, mythology says the Tritons who lived in a golden palace at the bottom of the sea often blew it at command of Neptune to soothe the restless waves."

"I have read that the largest of these trumpet shells are used as tea kettles by the people of the Typinsan Archipelago," said Mr. Bremely. "The shell has a wire or thong attached to each extremity, and is hung upon a hook above the fire. The operculum is the lid of this artistic tea kettle, while the spire serves as its spout."

"We might imagine sea gods resenting this common use of their 'wreathed horn,' and

"To the smooth, bright sand beguiled,

raising a 'tempest in the tea kettle,'" laughed Miss Bremely.

"On the contrary," replied her uncle, "I

fancy the shell that has been honored in mythology, painted by artists, and sung in poet's
lays, now appreciating the beauty there is in
homely use, and when the fire is on and the
water hot, sending forth sweeter songs than
when at the mouth of even Neptune's trumpeter himself."

The scientific name of this artistic tea kettle
is *Triton tritonis*.

Another variety, smaller but beautifully
variegated and mottled, is the *Triton variegatus*, whose habitat is the tropic sea in vicinity
of the Philippine Islands.

# SEA SECRETS.

When bearded mists divide,
Leave another's eyes and fetch your own.

EMERSON.

What swimmeth below
When the tide comes in ?

*Anon.*

# VI.

## SEA SECRETS.

Weeks passed quickly into months. Every hour was charmed.

Undine no longer spent the long golden days among her pillows, but with rounded cheeks and lips growing red as cherries she grew each week more and more like the rich roses and sun-kissed fruits of that happy valley. As for Tom, his interest in the sea and in ministers steadily deepened. He spent many hours upon the beach with ever-increasing delight, often in company with the new minister.

" Dr. McLean don't feed a fellow on the bare bones of wisdom," he assured Undine. "He tells just what one wants to know, and makes it so plain a poor chap like me understands what he's talking about. I'm s'prised that ministers know so much about such interesting things."

" Cousin makes things very plain, and tells

charming stories, too, about the sea," ventured Undine.

"Oh, course Cousin Ellen's nice," responded Tom; "but she can't go out and dig in the shoals and dredge and dip like the doctor."

Undine had no desire to depreciate their good friend, for she, like Tom, had learned to love him dearly, and was greatly interested in what he told them of the old sea's secrets.

Dr. McLean was a faithful pastor and a diligent student. His hours upon the strand were his recreation, and the little dip net and improvised dredge brought up for him many things other than *helices* and *hydroids*. To him the ocean with its vivid and changing pages was full of the thoughts of God, and he went down to its study reverently, with the thought in his heart, "The sea is his and he made it," and it thus became to him full of sweet sermonry.

To the boy and girl whose lessons had been tossed to them by the waves in the shape of shells and seaweeds, these implements—the dip net and the dredge—opened a new world of wonders. To the ignorant, the brine and mud in the trawl would have disclosed only wriggling bits of transparency, tiny beads of glass, opaque or shining, atoms of quicksilver, and wisps of nothingness; but science detected hydroids, delicate scalaria, worm cases, salpæ, infant scallops, and marvels of embroidered embryo known only to science. The most precious and promising of these in jars of sea water awaited honorable investigation, while as to the remainder, with a flat rock serving for their table, the three strained and stirred, magnified and marveled over the common looking sand and muddy looking mud, "the maximum of interest being reached," Cousin Ellen declared, "when a boy actually forgot the demands of his own stomach in investigating the stomach of a stomapod!"

When the auspicious day dawned in which the treasures waiting in their tanks of sea water were to give up their secrets, the teacher and the children sat at a long table with strainers, saucers, pincers, and microscopes before them, while expectation and delight were upon their faces.

After examining and explaining several minute organisms and admiring delicate and snow-white scalaria, so small as to tax the microscope and yet perfect in every convolution, "This," said the man of science, extricating from its muddy cradle an atom of transparency, "is the *Sapphirina ovatolanceolata*."

"Oh, please drop his baptismal name," interrupted Tom. "Can't see such a little chap if he has a whole alphabet piled up before him!"

When the small individual with the distinguished name was arranged for inspection the doctor explained: "It is one of the glow-worms that at night fringe the waves with gold or hang their lamps in the coral groves and the seaweed gardens." His listeners were eager for another of the fairy tales of science, and he continued: "Beautiful as are the ocean depths by the light of day, it is left for night to reveal marvels of beauty and brilliancy transcending the most vivid and gorgeous of earthly panoramas.

"It is not strange that fairy lore and tales of wonder ascribe to the sea charmed gardens and palaces glittering with gold and gems. Even their wealth of imagery fails to picture the brilliancy of the scene when under the canopy of night a strange carnival of light begins. The sea, then, has no dark and shadowy corners. Unattractive little brown beings scarcely noticed before, are changed as by magic into flowers of fire and fruit of gold upon the branching coral trees. Sea anemones hang their gorgeous blossoms over the reefs or wave their mimic rose-hued petals in what seems a gentle breeze. Dainty fronded 'sea ferns,' too delicate it would appear to bear their own weight, are strùng with what look like jeweled beads, or hung with infinitesimal electric lamps that burn and flash with intensest brilliancy.

"Under such floods of phosphorescent light the pink and purple of the seaweeds take on more vivid tints, and what was brown before grows rich-hued as tints of autumn are.

"Upon 'the diamond ledges that jut from these dells,' the self-luminous *Medusæ* and microscopic crustaceans seem signaling to each other by lights of every hue which flicker and wane but to flash again with brighter glow."

# A PORTUGUESE MAN-OF-WAR.

God hath so many ships upon the seas!
His are the merchantmen that carry treasures,
The men-of-war, all bannered gallantly,
The little fisher boats, and barks of pleasure—
On all this sea of time there is not one
That sailed without his glorious name thereon.
CARL SPENCER.


Beneath the sunlit wave she swims concealed
By her own brightness; only now revealed
To sage's eye that gazes with delight
On things invisible to vulgar sight.
DRUMMOND.

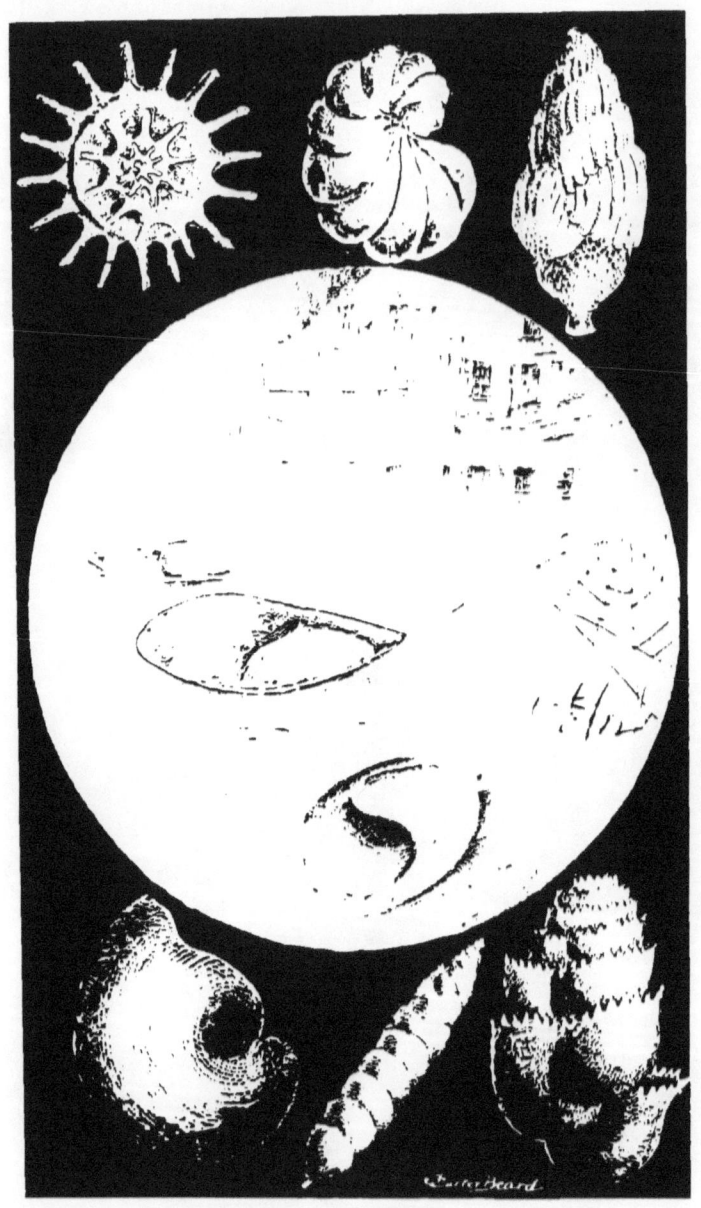

"One-seated shallops whose boatmen have departed."

## VII

## A PORTUGUESE MAN-OF-WAR.

*THE MEDUSÆ FAMILY.*

"A PORTUGUESE man-of-war has been stranded below on the beach," announced Mr. Bremely, one evening upon his return home. "It will pay you all to go down and see it."

Tom hastened to impart the information to Dr. McLean, who promised to join the excursion in the morning. He came and met Undine with the words: "I have brought a *Crepidula* in which to convey our Aphrodite to the scene of interest; it would be too long a walk for her."

Undine laughingly answered: "I know what a *Crepidula* is! I have some of the shells in my cabinet; they look like fairy boats with a seat in one end, and Cousin Ellen told me they had been called 'one-seated shallops whose boatmen had departed.' You mean I am to ride in something nice; but why call me Aphrodite? I don't know about that long word."

"Aphrodite," explained the doctor, "was a maiden lovely and loving, whom the old Greeks said sprang from the foam of the sea: her car was represented as drawn by a dove or a sparrow or sometimes a swan. Who or what will keep us company and be like the dove or the swan I'm sure I don't know."

"Cousin Ellen is like a dove," lovingly whispered Undine. Dr. McLean glanced across at the gentle lady in the soft gray gown, and the expression upon his face told that he agreed with Undine.

Tom questioned, "What kind of a boat is the Portuguese man-of-war? I can see neither steam nor sail along our beach," he added disappointedly.

"We shall find our craft none the less," replied Dr. McLean.

After passing down the beach for some distance Tom suddenly darted toward the water's edge, shouting: "The loveliest tangles of seaweed! All colors!"

"*Tom, stop! Don't touch that!*" exclaimed Dr. McLean in a voice so stern and commanding that Tom stopped at once, startled and troubled. He never had heard the minister speak with such severity before. Coming to Tom's side the party now saw a singularly beautiful object stranded, just low enough to be washed over by the waves. Long ribbon-like streamers and fringes, purple and rosy pink, floated out for yards beyond its richly colored body. Dr. McLean explained that the Portuguese man-of-war was a jellyfish belonging to the class *Acelephæ*, which means nettles, many members of this class possessing a stinging power which makes the name appropriate. "Tom," he continued, "those beautiful threadlike filaments, which at a glance you took for seaweeds, are filled with little cells, and each cell is a tiny armory where its death-dealing weapon is kept. If you had touched but one of those beautifully fringed appendages, even very softly, every little cell thus touched would have burst open, thrusting its poison-charged weapon into your flesh.

"These poison-filled tentacles are its weapons of defense and are also used in obtaining its food. The sea animal wounded by a sting from these lasso cells soon dies and is devoured by this singular creature.

"The home of the Portuguese man-of-war is in the tropics, and only occasionally does one drift so far into the colder currents. Another day we will return and see how much is left of this gay privateer.

"The whole *Medusæ* family are very curious and interesting, but none more so than the *Physalia*—our acquaintance of to-day," continued the doctor, losing no opportunity of instructing the children, who were delighted with the tales he told then. "Instances of the stinging powers of this inoffensive-looking creature are given, which show that Tom may congratulate himself that he was prompt in obeying orders. There is a story told of a young sailor who, attracted as Tom was by the beauty of this jellyfish, sprang into the sea to capture it as it passed near the ship. When he reached it the creature entangled him in its threadlike filaments; in an agony of pain he cried for help and had barely been drawn on to the vessel when the intensity of the inflammation produced by the stings of these tentacles occasioned brain fever.

"The different members of this family inhabit all seas. Some of them are very large, reaching to. two feet across the disk, with their tentacular appendages extending like threads of many colors; others of diminutive size float in immense shoals, and with their phosphorescence illumine the sea till every wave is 'a flash of golden fire.' There seems no end to the number and variety of these brilliant little creatures resembling drops of animated ice, tiny crystals of jelly, or floating jewels. Close study reveals in them organisms quite as marvelous as are possessed by sea beauties of larger growth. Some looking like translucent globules are furnished with bands of membranous fins or pellucid paddles whose ever-varying motion, under the play of light upon their glittering surfaces, gives them all the hues of a prism.

"Others are like fairy umbrellas of clearest crystal dotted with yellow specks along the margin; these the sages say are eyes. Fringing tentacles, more than a dozen times the length of the disk, float about them and shimmer like threads of fine-spun glass. To complete the fairylike umbrella the queer little stomach of the medusa hangs like a tiny handle from its center with the knoblike mouth at its extremity. Through the transparent canals we can see what this medusa had for breakfast and watch the process of digestion.

"The helpful lens enables us to trace the jellyfish through all its glittering transitions— from the egg or gemmule to the time when, tired of a sedentary, budding existence, it returns to the 'original type' and shoots off independently.

"The immense shoals of these microscopic animals not only help at night to produce what is called the 'phosphorescent sea,' but by the light of day give their color to the waves. Thus the variety known as 'whale food' redden the sea for miles, and when whalers perceive their ruddy hue upon the waves they realize they have reached the 'pastures of the whales.'"

By this time their walk had ended and Tom announced his "think tank full." When the party again visited the spot where they had left the Portuguese man-of-war, the children could find no trace of their singular acquaintance, and but for wiser companions would have returned home in disappointment. They were shown, however, several filmy objects, scarcely more than an inch across, flat, flabby, and semitransparent. These they learned were the air sacs of their jellyfish, and were told that even a medusa, weighing several pounds and with many yards of tentacles, when he dropped his "mortal coil" left only sea water and air sacs; these latter Tom presented to Undine as "the skeleton of the Portuguese man-of-war."

The colony of Hydroids growing about a truncated harp shell in our engraving gives a

HYDROIDS AND JELLY-FISH.

very good idea of the delicacy and beauty of some of these organisms, while above the Hydroids and the harp shell float what look like shimmering balloons, airy, fairy enough to bear "sylphs and fays beyond the moon."

These are jellyfish—*Medusæ*—first produced as buds upon the Hydroid, where they enlarge, until at length they become detached and float away.

Some Hydroids cast upon our sea beaches and preserved in collections might be taken for seaweeds, they are so delicate, were it not for their horny external coverings.

# PEARLS.—MOTHER-OF-PEARL.

6

The cockelle, with heavenly dew so clene
Of kynde, engendereth white pearls rounde.

*Old poem.*

When we see such forms as these we hardly like to
think that they are secreted by some slimy mollusk, but
would imagine that the mermaids tear off pieces of the
rainbows where they touch the sea, and carry them to the
cold depths to congeal them into shells.—*H. A. Ward's
Catalogue of Species.*

60

## VIII.

### PEARLS.—MOTHER-OF-PEARL.

FASCINATING as was microscopic study, Tom lost none of his admiration for the abalones, so lustrous and iridescent, while Undine looked for seed pearls in every bivalve that came into her hands.

Dr. McLean told them the pearly lining of the abalones was called mother-of-pearl, or *nacre*, while true pearls were the product of different bivalves, the best "solidified drops of dew," as the Orientals call them—being found in the pearl oyster (*Avicula margari-tifera*).

"According to an ancient fable," continued the doctor, "oysters rose to the surface of the water, opened their shells, and received the drops of dew which were speedily transformed to 'white pearls rounde.' In recognition of this fable Thomas Moore wrote:

"Precious their tears as rain from the sky
That turns into pearls as it falls in the sea.

"Another theory has been that pearls were always the result of a grain of sand or some irritating substance entering the shell; the animal, unable to discharge it, converted it into a pearl. Hence we are told :

"Learn from yon Orient shell to love thy foe,
    And strew with pearls the hand that brings thee woe.

This is beautifully suggestive, yet seems to be only half the story. While irritating substances are known to be covered by *nacre* it is believed all pearls are not the result of irritation, but are secreted by the mollusk and held ready to be dissolved by powerful acids, which are also of the animal's secretion, for spreading over openings made in their shells by the borer.

"Injured shells are often found with their points of irritation covered with thin laminations of this nacreous matter.

"Pearl fishers tell us the little pearl maker is, sometimes at least, able to expel his jewel at will, and often does so when captured ; understanding this, the fisher places his hand over the shell so as to close its valves or secure the pearl if ejected.

"After possessing himself of all the pearls in old mussels—the old being the most productive—the gatherer sometimes deposits the mol-

lusks in safe and convenient coves where he
may gather the pearls for several years in suc-
cession from the same shells.

"The Chinese, understanding the ability of
these pearl mussels to cover hard substances
with their fluid secretion, which soon hardens
into mother-of-pearl, or *nacre*, bring their wiles
to bear upon a species of fresh-water mussel—
the *Unio Hyria*—compelling it to manufacture
pearls to their order.

"They keep the little *Unio* in tanks, and
place small shot, bits of shell, and other substances between the mantle and the valve;
these particles are soon converted into pearls
by the industrious little gem maker.

"They carry their 'ways that are dark'
still further, and by means of the work of
the innocent little *Unio* they impose upon
the credulous and superstitious minds of their
people. They insert a metal image of their
god Buddha within the valves of the mussel,
and in process of time it becomes coated with
the nacreous secretion and—presto!—the image of Buddha in pearl and adhering to the
shell of a mussel! The image commands a
good price and promises great advantage to the
ignorant dupe who sees in it an unanswerable
affirmation of Buddha's divinity.

"The pearl oyster which produces the finest pearls of all the pearl-growing bivalves is found at considerable depth in large shoals in the Indian Ocean, Gulf of Persia, some parts of the Pacific Ocean, etc. About thirty thousand people find employment in the pearl fisheries of the Persian Gulf alone.

"As many as one hundred and fifty pearls have been gathered from a single shell.

"Among the other bivalves producing pearls is the *Pinna* or wing-shell, the valves of which are often two feet long; the best known variety is the *P. nobilis*, which inhabits the Mediterranean, and is especially curious on account of its byssus.

"Another singular variety is the hammer oyster—*Malleus vulgaris*—whose hammer-shaped shell is beautifully laminated with mother-of-pearl.

"But Tom must hear about his beautiful abalones," said the doctor, seeing he held several in his hands.

"This rainbow shell belongs to the family *Haliotidæ*, of which there are many species, named according to their slight variations and the localities which they inhabit.

"Abalone—the name which we upon this California coast familiarly use—is a name the

PEARL-PRODUCING SHELLS.

early Spanish settlers gave, and is of doubtful meaning.

"Shells of this family have their center of distribution in Australian and adjacent seas. Quantities abound upon the coast of Japan, where they are known as '*Awabi.*' Other names by which they are often called are ear-shell, green ear, Omer shell, etc.

"*Haliotis splendens* and *H. tuberculata* are the names science has given to the beauties you have in your hands, Tom.

"An enormous traffic is carried on in these shells so useful in delicate inlaying, in lacquer, and other ornamental work. The animals inhabiting these palaces are considerably sought after for food, while fine pearls have been found within the mantle of some. The iridescent tints of these shells are produced by the fluid secretion with which the interior of the shells are lined; this hardens quickly and becomes *nacre*, presenting a beautifully smooth and polished surface to the tender body of the animal within. They are also due to the excessively thin laminations, irregularly overlapping, laid on in delicate semitransparent films. The thinner the laminations of this nacre membrane the more transparent, and hence the more lustrous and beautiful, the shell.

"You are aware, Tom, with what tenacity these abalones cling to the rocks, so they can only be removed by taking the little householder unawares and giving dextrous and sudden knocks."

"Yes," said Tom, "the people here tell of a Chinaman who, putting his fingers under one of these shells in his attempt to pry it from the rock, was held there by the abalone until the tide came up and the man was drowned."

"This tight hugging of the rock," explained the doctor, "is accounted for, I believe, by the large suckerlike sole of the animal. It consists of a rounded disk of muscular tissue, which has marvelous power of adhesion and brings not a little atmospheric pressure to bear upon the shell. Like the limpet, it has a very viscous secretion, which is a strong factor in holding it to the rock.

"The apertures along its dome suggest round windows high up in some old castle wall. They are the openings through which the gills of the animal are kept in communication with the surrounding water. The earlier openings you see are closed—filled up with shelly matter—but some are always kept open."

As the doctor laid down the abalones, Un-

dine, with a womanly penchant for the dainty
and delicate, reverted to pearls, twirling the
while a ring upon her finger and displaying
the soft luster, the purity, and slight transparency of its pearly setting. "I have read," she
said, " that Cleopatra once dissolved and drank
a pearl. In the story she was called very beautiful, but I can not see how a woman so fool-
ish and vain could have been very beautiful."

"Yet it is true," replied Dr. McLean;
"her beauty and power to charm so influ-
enced rulers and warriors that it has been said
if Cleopatra's nose had been half an inch longer
(so spoiling her beauty) the history of the
world would have been different!

"Nevertheless science is not a little skep-
tical about the pearl which it is recorded she
dissolved and drank. It was one of a pair and
was valued at one hundred and fifty thousand
golden crowns. It is now affirmed upon excellent authority that so large a pearl could not
have been dissolved except by means of a powerful acid, and so large a quantity would have
been required that it could never have been
drank with impunity.

"The mate to this pearl, so the authorities
say, was sawn in twain by order of the Em-
peror Severus and dedicated to Venus, being

used in decorating her statue in the Parthenon.

" Nevertheless the dissolving and drinking of such a costly draught would scarcely have surpassed the extravagancies indulged in by the ancient nations of wealth. Fabulous sums were paid for pearls, and they were used with greatest prodigality. Whole crowns were made of them ; idols and images were studded and encrusted with them; and they were wrought into the most delicate and beautiful of fabrics. The earliest records concerning the use of gems among the ancient Babylonians, Egyptians, and Persians show that pearls were regarded as among the richest gifts of Nature. By the Romans the mania for their possession was even greater.

" Mithradates, the formidable opponent of the Romans, as you were reading this morning, was also not only a lover of wars, but a considerable lover of the arts as well. When he was conquered by Pompey and his magnificent collection of gems was taken, quantities of pearls were found, some of them wrought into most exquisite and elaborate designs. Among them was a portrait of the king himself cunningly fashioned entirely of pearls in mosaic.

" The settings of your ring, Undine," said

the doctor, seeing the little girl still twirling
the pearls upon her finger, "are white and lustrous and have the polish that pertains to the
very finest pearls. It has been suggested that
this wonderful polish and perfection of luster
which art can not imitate, may have been caused
by the continued friction of the soft body of
the oyster.

"We hold such pearls as these in the highest esteem, but, since there is no accounting for
tastes, we find the inhabitants of some other
countries differ from us in their estimation of
these gems. We have been accustomed to
think of pearls as white alone, and we have
thought of them as Nature's expression of
purity. This is not the case with all admirers
of pearls. The people of India and of China,
for example, see greater beauty in those of a
bright yellow color, while others prefer those
that are pink. Pink pearls, as they are called,
are not all pink, but range in hue from pink to
red or even pale yellow or a dull dead white.
They are generally neither very beautiful nor
very perfect. Others of a black or leaden-gray
color are also sometimes met with, and when
perfect and of a good shape are highly valued.

"As you already know, the Pacific Ocean
yields a rich harvest of these gems, and it

seems highly probable that the regions of California and Panama were known to the ancient inhabitants of America as rich fisheries. The hearts of Cortes and his followers were fired with anticipation and with envy when they saw the wealth of gems, many of them pearls, with which the draperies of the wealthy Aztecs were embroidered and fringed, and their gold and feather work sprinkled with jewels. By the conquests of the Spaniards in Mexico and Peru great quantities of pearls were obtained. Old Spanish historians have recorded wonderful stories of the wealth of the Aztec kings in pearls, immense numbers of which were exceedingly fine. They also affirm the familiarity of these people with the localities from which they were obtained."

# FLOWERS OF THE SEA.

No words that I know of will say what these mosses are—none are delicate enough, none perfect enough, none rich enough. . . . The traceries of intricate silver and fringes of amber, lustrous, arborescent, burnished through every fiber into fitful brightness and glossy traverses of silken change, yet all subdued and pensive, and framed for simplest, sweetest offices of grace.—RUSKIN.

Hearts there are on the sounding shore,
   Something whispers soft to me,
Restless and roaming forevermore,
   Like this, the weary weed of the sea;
Bear they yet on each beating breast
   The eternal type of the wondrous whole,
Grace unfolding amid unrest,
   Grace informing with silent soul.
                                C. G. FENNER.

72

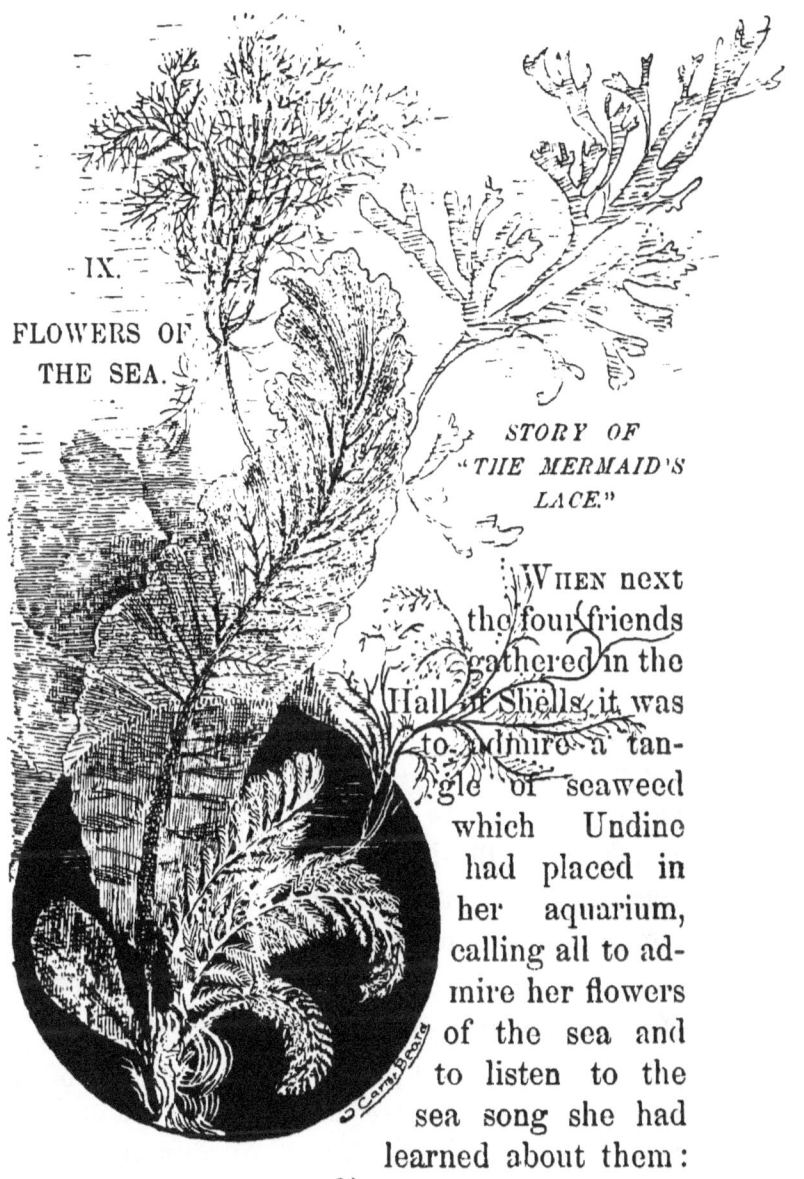

## IX.

### FLOWERS OF THE SEA.

*STORY OF "THE MERMAID'S LACE."*

WHEN next the four friends gathered in the Hall of Shells, it was to admire a tangle of seaweed which Undine had placed in her aquarium, calling all to admire her flowers of the sea and to listen to the sea song she had learned about them:

73

On the surface, foam and roar,
　　Restless heave and passion dash,
Shingle rattle along the shore,
　　Gathering boom and thundering crash.

Under the surface loveliest forms,
　　Feathery fronds with crimson curl,
Treasures too deep for the raid of storms—
　　Delicate coral and hidden pearl.

.　　　.　　　.　　　.　　　　.　　　.

These, the strands of a carpet soft,
　　Richer than mortal ever trod;
Freed by the current and borne aloft
　　To show us the hidden work of God.

She begged Dr. McLean to tell of these delicate sea flowers. He began by saying: "The term *Algæ*, or seaweeds, is much more restricted than formerly; it used to embrace many marine specimens now consigned to the animal kingdom. Many are the gay dissemblers in the sea, and we can almost imagine them laughing together at their successes in so long deceiving the very elect of scientists.

"Linnæus, a Swedish naturalist, with great love for Nature and great skill in guessing her riddles, was one of the first to see that many so-called sea plants were sensitive to human touch, and possessed the organs of animal life. He catalogued fifty species which he regarded as seaweeds; we now know of several thousand, though our knowledge of many of these is quite limited.

"*Algæ* have been regarded as belonging to one of three classes, according to their color: the *Melanospermeæ* embraced the olive brown and black; the *Rhodospermeæ* were the purple and the red; while the *Chlorospermeæ* were the green. This arrangement has been discarded and various others substituted, relating more particularly to the structure and development of the *Algæ*. These classifications, however, are still very imperfect, and the nomenclature of many groups is still undetermined. Whether man understands and gives them a name or not, they grow in grace and beauty, perfectly understood by their Creator and accomplishing his will.

"They draw their sustenance from the water, being without roots, often fastening themselves by a kind of sucker to rocks, shells, and sea bottoms. Not unfrequently their hold becomes loosened or their branches broken, so we find them tossed by the waves upon the strand or carried in tangles through the waters, far from their native colonies. So great are these masses as sometimes to hinder the passage of ships in their courses. Varieties of kelp in vicinity of the Falkland Islands are

7

twisted by the waves into enormous vegetable
cables several hundred feet long and thicker
than the human body. There are bays where
thousands of people have found employment
gathering these spoils after an ocean storm.

"The *Sargassum bacciferum* is the Gulf
weed, which always floats and is not unfamil-
iar to voyagers upon the Atlantic and Pacific
Oceans. The localities where this seaweed is
most abundant are called Sargasso Seas.

"Seaweeds love best the quiet waters of
the temperate seas, avoiding the cold waves of
the frigid zones and the more heated currents
of the torrid. If found in these, they lack the
delicacy of the mosses in the temperate zone.
Different seas and different localities have their
distinct sea flora, often found in such immense
colonies as to give their color to the sea.

"They are dependent upon light, hence
are not found below one thousand feet, or
the depth to which light ceases to penetrate.
Light is their painter also: mosses near the
surface, catching its fullest rays, are green
like terrestrial vegetation; the brilliant reds
and delicate pinks are to be found upon rocks
at no great depth and near the coasts; those
in the deeper seas grow brown and abundant,
and their somber hues but enhance the bril-

liancy of those that have enjoyed more of the kisses of the sun. They wave like plumes, like gayest ribbons are tossed in the currents; some as fine as frostwork can scarcely be discerned, while others in mimic forests grow to a thousand feet."

Miss Bremely remarked: "There is one variety of seaweed which has passed into history because of its influence upon the industry and the lives of a far-away people. Shall I tell you about it?" She read her answer in the eager faces turned toward her; that of the good doctor beamed with especial pleasure as he listened, and Undine wondered that she had not known before that Dr. McLean liked seaweeds so well.

### "THE MERMAID'S LACE."

The little island of Burano lies like a gem in the blue Adriatic. In the early days its inhabitants were simple fisher folk, spreading their nets at night in the coves of the sea; in the morning, carrying their fish in rude gondolas to the markets of Venice. The women mended the broken nets or netted new ones, little guessing they were catching a trick of netting which should one day form the foundation of a fabric to be the pride of royalty.

But all were not content with this quiet island life. There was one, a youth, who heard strange voices in his soul, luring him away from this little anchorage. The great world, that drew him with a power he could not resist, prepared a bark for him she called, and he went out, not knowing whither he went.

At last, in the far south seas, his heart bade him tear from its briny fastness an unknown seaweed whose beauty attracted him strangely. He had sailed far for this unknown plant.

As our hearts prompt us to bestow upon our best beloved the most beautiful gifts at our command, so the heart of this man, who was performing a mission, though he knew it not, bade him carry this trophy of his voyage to a maiden who waited in far Burano.

With the utmost care he preserved the delicate *Algæ*, and after weeks long and many of weary sailing, he laid the plant, perfect and beautiful, in the hand of the waiting maiden.

But, alas! there came a day when the treasure began to fade; and the maiden saw that, notwithstanding her greatest effort, her gift must perish. The same spirit that prompted to its gathering inspired the little fisherwoman.

THE MERMAID'S LACE.

Tirelessly she worked, matching the skill her fingers had acquired in netting of seines with a quenchless desire to preserve a semblance of her fair but perishable treasure.

Finally there dawned a morning when the plant lay black and withered. All the beauty which had held the two hearts by its magic was gone ; but in the hand of the maiden lay its delicate counterpart, woven of the finest of threads.

The little sea plant which, it is said, actually furnished designs for the original Venetian point lace, the netting of which the women of Burano and of Venice were anciently so famous, has since been known as mermaid's lace.

# THE ARGONAUT.—THE NAUTILUS.

A bevy of roses, apple-cheeked,
In a shell of crystal, ivory-beaked,
With a satin sail of a ruby glow.

EMERSON.

The winds go up and down upon the seas,
And some they lightly clasp, entreating kindly,
And waft them to the port where they would be ;
And other ships they buffet, long and blindly,
And God hath many wrecks within the sea.
Yet it is sweet to think his care is under,
That yet the sunken treasure may be drawn
Into his storehouse when the sea is gone.

CARL SPENCER.

82

## X.

### THE ARGONAUT.—THE NAUTILUS.

The day following, Dr. McLean brought Undine a large translucent shell; so thin and shining was it as to suggest the possibility of its vanishing in air like a bubble.

"Yesterday," he said, placing the shell in her hand, "your cousin told us how a people learned to make lace from a piece of seaweed. I will tell you how the *Argonauta* taught men navigation.

"The argonaut and nautilus, although both belonging to the cephalopods—the highest division of the mollusks—are in most points quite unlike; yet in consequence of a similarity in the form of their shells their names have often been indiscriminately used. The little voyager with the silken sail is the *Argonauta Argo*, quite generally known as paper nautilus.

"Many and charming are the stories told of this little sailor who, in his fairy bark with satin sail, was wafted o'er the 'unshadowed main.' Six of its arms it dropped as oars at the side of its shallop and two more with their membranes of silk were spread to the wind.

"It is said that catching glimpses of this little mariner with whose inner life, it now appears, the ancients had no very intimate acquaintance, they conceived the idea of the vessels which they constructed, propelled by oars, or wafted by the winds. The steamer, too, was an outgrowth of hints given by these little cephalopods, who by forcing water violently through a tube in the body drive themselves with considerable speed in a backward direction.

"Pictures of these little mariners sailing in fairy fleets have fascinated the world from Aristotle down, and we can hardly pardon scientists of the present day who compel to the belief that these stories are but charming myths. The pretty fleets the ancients saw, we are told, were probably not *Nautili* at all, but were the *Argonauta*, which are true floating mollusks; but even these we are now informed never row their tiny craft nor spread a topsail.

"The 'arms' of these little animals, we must now believe, were held during the voyage close to the side of the 'sharp-keeled, high-pooped' little vessel 'to keep its balance

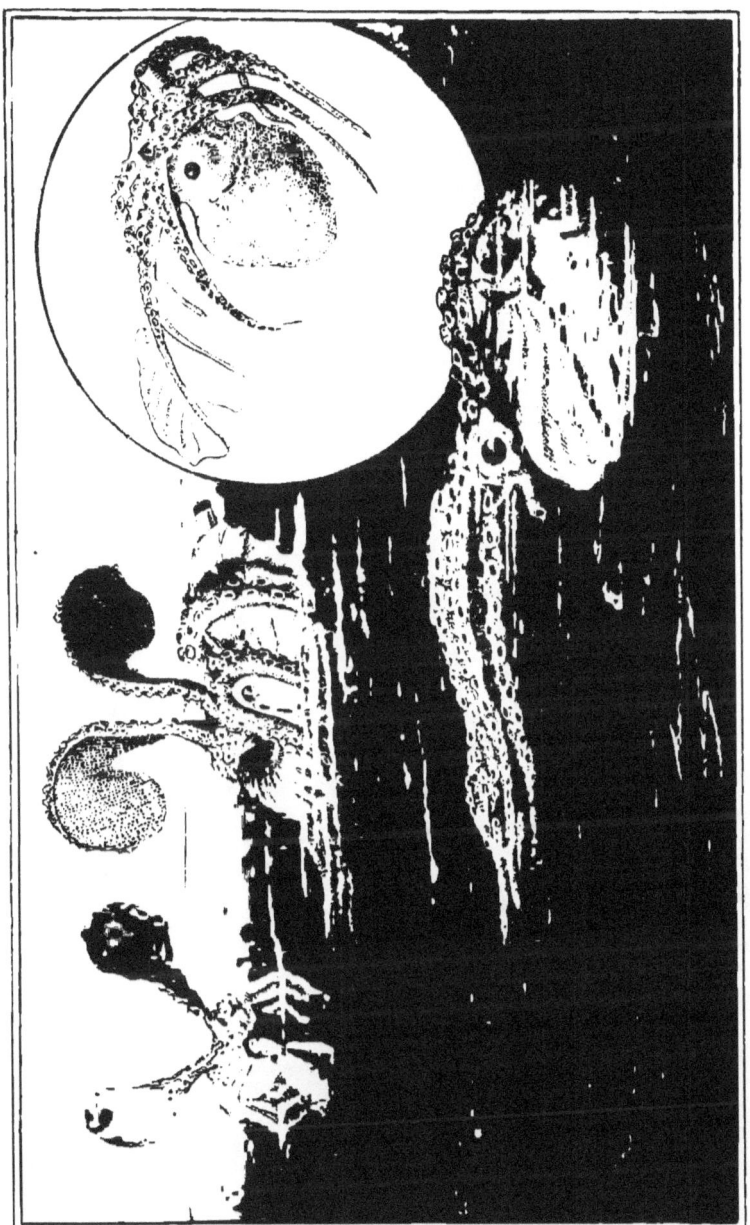

THE ARGONAUT.

straight,' while the two winglike membranes,
that we loved to think were silvery sails, are
now supposed to be the secreting organs used
in fabricating the boat of pearl.  These wise
observers have found, too, that it is only the
female argonaut who rides like a princess, the
males being diminutive and possessed of no
insignia of royalty.

"The little princess sits serenely in her
shell, but is in no way attached to it, and might
unharmed be lifted out and placed in another.

"The shell, besides serving as her boat, is
the pearly cradle or little ark in which the
infant *Argonauta* are borne in safety through
the floods.  The eggs are fastened to filamen-
tary stalks and by these to the involuted spire
of the shell, and are usually concealed by the
body of the mother.

"This shell of the argonaut as you see,"
said the doctor, reverting to the shell which
Undine still held in her hand, "is thin and
brittle as glass; hence while thousands sail the
seas but few are found upon the shores.

"On the contrary, the shell of the nautilus
is thick and strong, and found upon many
tropic shores.  The pearly nautilus is the one
with which we are best acquainted, and seems
to be the most abundant.  This shell is some-

times a foot across, delicately porcelainlike, of
a light-buff tint, beautifully veined or striped
in a zigzag pattern with chestnut brown. The
beauty of the nacreous lining of this shell I
have no words to describe. It seems a mingling of the delicate tints of most delicate
flowers and the beauty and brilliancy of rarest
gems.

"The shell is divided into chambers, hence
the name 'chambered nautilus.' When very
young this is not the case, but as the animal
increases in size it leaves its first compartment,
which becomes an empty chamber, and moves
forward to one still larger; the rim of the shell
continues to grow, and back of the little occu-
pant a pearly partition is produced. This is
repeated from time to time, the little animal
always using the room next to the vestibule;
but through all preserving a connection by
means of a silvery membranous tube called a
siphuncle.

" But few species of these animals now re-
main and they alone in warm seas, but geology
shows that both *Argonauta* and *Nautili* were
very abundant in earlier periods.

"The fossil ammonite was a kind of 'old-
fashioned cousin' to the nautilus or paper
sailor. These are found in great abundance,

some rocks being composed almost entirely of
them. The name ammonite comes from a word
meaning ram, as anciently these shells were
thought to be ram's horns, which, indeed, they
do resemble; hence popularly called *Cornua
Ammonis*, Jupiter Ammon, an Egyptian deity,
being sometimes represented in old sculptures
with head and horns of a ram, these latter and
the shells bearing a fancied resemblance.

"They have also been taken by the ignorant for petrified snakes and called 'serpent
stones.' The ignorant have been further de-
luded by having these 'serpent stones' presented to them with a finely carved snake's
head at one end of the coil, while a cunningly
devised tradition accounted for the general absence of the head upon the ground that a saint
had first beheaded the reptiles and afterward
changed them into stone. Sir Walter Scott
weaves this legend into his poem entitled Mar-
mion, when close around the fire

> " Whitby's nuns exulting told
> How, of thousand snakes, each one
> Was changed into a coil of stone,
> When holy Hilda prayed.

And how

> " Themselves, within their holy bound,
> Their stony folds had often found.

"These 'stony folds,' or fossil shells, are sometimes found three and four feet in diameter, but the majority are much smaller. The smaller chambers of these shells seem also to have been air cells, all connected by means of the tube through which air was forced in or dispelled, enabling the little animal to rise or sink at pleasure. These pearly partitions also served to strengthen the shell.

"But our story is incomplete," said the doctor, "without that charming poem which has given to Dr. Holmes the title of 'Poet Laureate of the Nautilus.'"

Miss Bremely, who had anticipated this wish and sat with book in hand, now read the following poem entitled

THE CHAMBERED NAUTILUS.

This is the ship of pearl that poets feign
Sails the unshadowed main,
The venturous bark that flings
On the sweet summer wind its purple wings
In gulfs enchanted, where the siren sings
And coral reefs lie bare,
Where the cold sea-maids rise to sun their streaming hair.

Its webs of living gauze no more unfurl,
Wrecked is the ship of pearl
And every chambered cell,
Where its dim dreaming life was wont to dwell,
As the frail tenant shaped his growing shell,

Before thee lies revealed—
Its irised ceiling rent, its sunless crypt unsealed.


Year after year beheld the silent toil
That spread this lustrous coil,
Still as the spiral grew,
He left the last year's dwelling for the new,
Stole with soft step its shining archway through,
Built up its idle door,
Stretched in its last found home and knew the old no
    more.


Thanks for the heavenly message brought from thee,
Child of the wandering sea,
Cast from her lap, forlorn !
From thy dead lips a clearer note is borne
Than ever Triton blew from wreathèd horn !
While on my ear it rings,
Through the deep caves of thought I hear a voice that
    sings.


Build thee more stately mansions, O my soul,
As the swift seasons roll,
Leave thy low-vaulted past !     .
Let each new temple, nobler than the last,
Shut thee from heaven with a dome more vast
Till thou at length art free,
Leaving thy outgrown shell by life's unresting sea.

# ROCKED IN THE CRADLE OF THE DEEP.

8

The sea is a jovial comrade,
    He laughs wherever he goes;
His merriment shines in the dimpling lines
    That wrinkle his hale repose;
He lays himself down at the feet of the sun,
    And shakes all over with glee,
And the broad-backed billows fall faint on the shore,
    In the mirth of the mighty sea!

BAYARD TAYLOR.

92

## XI

ROCKED IN THE CRADLE OF THE DEEP.

"How happy the sea looks to-day! Its waves are sparkling and dimpling as with merriment," and Undine's heart was like the sea of which she spoke.

"Halloo!" shouted Tom from the water's edge; "here's something beats a mermaid's cradle. It's funny enough to make old Neptune roar." And Tom's laughter, though perhaps a trifle less uproarious, was a very good substitute.

There lay a clam shell upon the sand. The tide had lifted a diminutive crab into it and left both just low enough for the sea to touch with its silvery hands and keep them rocking.

"That might be called crabbed comfort," laughed Miss Bremely, "and looks as if Venus had turned Crustacean baby tender."

After amusing themselves for some time over what Tom called "a freak of Nature," the ever-observant Undine asked, "Cousin Ellen,

what did you mean by saying that about
Venus turning Crustacean baby tender?"

"The shell in which the baby crab is rocking is called *Venus Californiensis*," said her
cousin, "and all the shells of this family were
long ago dedicated to the sea-born maiden
Venus, whom the doctor told you about some
time ago, only he called her Aphrodite, the
name the old Greeks gave her. Many of the
shells of this family are among the most beautifully colored and sculptured as well as the
most graceful in shape, and as such were regarded fitting offerings to the goddess who was
said to surpass all others in grace and beauty.

"Clams of different varieties are abundant
in salt water, some with shells heavy and
rough, others thin almost to transparency and
beautifully tinted. The round clam, known on
the Atlantic coast as quahog and valued as
an article of food, furnished the famous purple
wampum from the margin of its shell. This
violet wampum was counted twice as valuable
as the white by the aborigines, and its money
value has been commemorated in the name *V.
mercenaria*, by which this clam is called.

"The solid shells of the surf clam, *Mactra
solidissima*, were used by the same Indians as
hoes for cultivating their maize fields.

"The giant clam, *Tridacna gigas*, would make a 'sliding chariot' large enough for a very good-sized sea nymph. This shell, which is said to be the largest in the world, has been found with its valves nearly two yards long and weighing over five hundred pounds. Should you ever go to Paris and visit the Church of St. Sulpice you will there see two valves of this tridacna which are used for holding 'holy water.'

"One of the most elegant bivalves is that tridacna known as 'bear's paw.' It is from the Indian Ocean, and is beautifully mottled with yellow and red.

"These are only a few of the many varieties of clams suggested by this cradle rocking in the waves. All do not belong to the Venus family, howsoever much by their beauty they may deserve the honor."

Tom had compared the rocking clam shell to a "mermaid's cradle." In her hall of shells Undine had a dainty chiton, the *C. Katherina*, of which she was very fond. It was really a gem of a cradle.

The chitons are curious specimens when alive, and death invests them with charms which in life they failed to possess. The shell is made up of eight different pieces so united by strong ligaments as to allow of the animal adapting itself to rounding surfaces or even to roll itself up like a ball. This skeleton is the pretty " mermaid's cradle."

Icelandic sailors affirm the not very palatable-looking chiton if swallowed will allay seasickness or quench thirst.

We have heard of no one able to refute this statement, and in our heart of hearts seriously doubt if any one, even in the pangs of seasickness, ever attempted the experiment.

# GAY, SAD SCHEVENINGEN.

The very waves that washed the sand
  Below him he had seen before
Whitening the Scandinavian strand
  And sultry Mauritanian shore,
From ice-rimmed isles, from summer seas
Palm-fringed, they brought him messages.
                            WHITTIER.

                        . . . but yet
I feel for mariners of stormy nights,
And feel for wives that watch ashore.  Ay, ay,
If I had learning I would pray the Lord
  To bring them in.
But I make bold to say, " O Lord, good Lord,
I am a broken-down poor man, a fool
To speak to thee.  But in the book 'tis writ,
As I hear say from others that can read,
How when thou camest thou didst love the sea,
And live with fisher folk, whereby 'tis sure
Thou knowest all the peril they go through
And all their trouble."
                            JEAN INGELOW.

## GAY, SAD SCHEVENINGEN.

WHEN Dr. McLean again called, he found the party at the beach; upon joining them Undine was quick to spy a package of shells he brought.

"These are for you, little Sea-Maiden," he said, "and will whisper you runes from the north, for they came from Scheveningen upon the stormy North Sea."

"Oh, strange Scheveningen!" exclaimed Miss Bremely. "Do tell the children of that curious place."

So Dr. McLean told them of Schevenin-gen, where Holland steps down into the sea, where the sands pile themselves into dunes. Gay throughout the summer with the beautiful, the wealthy, the titled, and the crowned of Europe; beaten in winter by the wind-lashed, wraith-whispering, jötun-vexed sea.

He told of its independent, ingenious, and curiously isolated people; of their little village of black cottages over against their other village of gay and fashionable dwellings; but two miles from The Hague, yet as distinct and original as if from another continent.

He led the little group to respect and admire the sturdy industry and independence which wove such strong fiber in the characters of these secluded, oddly dressed, and extremely poor people.

He told them how in the decline of the herring fishing, which had been their chief industry, the people were not discouraged, but in rope spinning, weaving nets, gathering shells, selling fish, and the like, gaining but the scantiest of living, were still brave and true, their very poverty invigorating their characters. How in eye and bearing they demand respect, and with dignity seem to say, "We have need of none!" He told them of the sand dunes, and of the broad beach of hard sand, dotted over with tents and wickerlike chairs with woven covers, to shelter from the sun; of the unique arrangement for bathers; of the festivals and gayeties in which the flower of the aristocracy of Europe participate.

When he had finished, and the children were busy upon the beach, he continued musingly, half to himself and half to Miss Bremely:

"Brave, brave Scheveningen! Gay, sad Scheveningen! As thou hast two villages, so thou hast two lives! The festivals of summer pass, but none save Heaven and the dwellers in the little black cottages know the heart tragedies enacted there, 'the mortal anxieties, the holy joy of return, and the inconsolable sorrow of parting.'

"There is," he continued, "a Scheveningen memory which these shells always suggest to me."

Seeing Miss Bremely's interest, he related as follows:

"I had been in The Hague two weeks and had often met at my hotel a French count, for whom I instinctively felt an extreme aversion. I had also often seen an Austrian party, evidently people of rank. There was nothing particularly attractive about any of these people, except one, a lady quite young and the most lilylike of any person I had ever beheld. Her complexion was fair as that delicate flower, with a certain charm suggesting to me nothing so much as a lily. Her every motion was replete with grace, and her hair, which curled in rings about her face, was like sunlit gold, always reminding me of Mrs. Browning's words,

"How many golden scudi
Went to make such ringlets.

"I knew nothing whatever concerning her, but was attracted by her beauty, as old tales tell us men have been charmed by the beauty of a siren.

"In my wanderings about the city I often sauntered into a shop where curiosities were sold. I was interested in the relics displayed, which were of an exceptionally fine order, but more, I think, I liked while looking at his wares to listen to the talk of the garrulous old man, who delighted in leaning over his counter and telling the stranger of people and places in his beloved fatherland.

"His face radiated good humor, and kindness was written in its every line. One day while studying some fine pictures of Holland scenery, Herr Witzman, for that was the old vender's name, interrupted me with exclamations of delight at the beautiful horses he saw dashing down the street. Upon looking out I saw they were attached to a tiny *voiture*, and were driven by the count of my aversion, while at his side sat the lilylike lady with the golden curls.

"I had but time to perceive this when,

'*Mein Gott! Mein Gott! Es ist Emilie!*' came from the lips of Herr Witzman.

"The dashing horses seemed poised in air, their feet almost upon the head of one of the strangest looking beings I had ever seen, one whose peculiar costume showed her to be a woman of Scheveningen. The feet of the horses descended and the human creature lay crushed beneath them.

"The count uttered an exclamation of anger, and lashing the fiery horses dashed on down the street, while the lilylike lady, only whiter grown, with a little scream nestled closer to the side of the count.

"The poor, mangled, broken piece of humanity was tenderly lifted by the old curiosity vender himself and carried into his little shop, while again he repeated, '*Mein Gott! Es ist Emilie!*'

"Upon nearer view, and with the strange hat which she had worn removed, I saw the woman's face, though marked by toil and exposure, was finely chiseled. Its lines of character were drawn strong and deep. I instinctively compared her face with that of the lilylike maiden, and found I regarded the latter as I had regarded the count. Her beauty was gone forever.

"A physician was summoned and restora-
tives applied, but Emilie, as her good old
friend called her, was past the help of man.
She revived somewhat, but knew none and was
unconscious of the presence of any about her,
but with wavering breath talked to one we
could not see.

"'Are the boats in?' she whispered, her
rugged native speech sweet with solicitude.
'It has been long waiting—so long!' Then
wearily she seemed to sleep.

"Again she whispered, 'The fog—the fog
—Heaven help the—boats—if they be—coming
in!' Then after a pause, '*Mutter*—list for the
—signals of—*Der Leitstern*. The roaring—of
the sea—is—in—my ears. It is—very cold.'
A shudder passed over her frame; it would
have been taken for a paroxysm of pain but
that she was past pain's cruel power. When
she spoke again it was hurriedly, as with joy,
but with great weakness. 'God be praised!' she
said; '*Der Leitstern*—is coming—through—the
fog! It shines—*Mutter*—like a—star. Heinrich!—God be praised!—Heinrich—beckons—
at the prow! See—*Mutter*—how grand—and
fair—he looks! Heinrich—calls—us! Haste,
*Mutter*—I—will—help—thee. The—boat—is
—here. Heinrich—I—come! God—be——'

"We who watched doubted not her ejaculation of praise and thanksgiving was finished just beyond our dull ears' hearing, and the hand she raised with her last fluttering heart beat was laid in the hand of him she saw 'so grand and fair' waiting for her upon the phantom ship.

"When all was over Herr Witzman told me Emilie's sad story.

"Eighteen years before *Der Leitstern* sailed away to fish for herring on the seas about Scotland. No braver, truer man sailed with her than Heinrich Bretzel, to whom Emilie was betrothed and to whom she should be wed when the flotilla returned from its fishing cruise.

"Scarcely a week after the boats went out a fearful storm came on ; the heavens were black for days, and the angry sea below seemed rising to meet the angry sky above. *Der Leitstern* was never seen again nor its crew heard from. But knowing the character and habits of the Scheveningen fishermen, we believe that after doing their utmost, then, as their custom is, they shut every aperture of the boats, and going into the cabin read the words of him who 'ruleth the raging of the sea' and waited his will.

"When the boats came no more, Emilie, who

was not needed in the cottage of her parents,
went to the lone mother of her betrothed and
labored for her support. When there were no
fish for her to bring to the markets of The
Hague, she came to Herr Witzman with shells
she gathered among the sad waves at Scheveningen. The day of which I have told you she
had a small store of shells and was evidently
crossing to Herr Witzman's little shop when
thrown under the feet of the horses.

"I bought the shells, giving their price into
the hand of Herr Witzman to be used toward
her burial. The day following I was myself
at Scheveningen.

"I sat in one of the wicker-basket chairs
upon the wide sand beach when a curious
closed carriage drawn by a single strong horse
came down the sand and was driven out far
into the sea. A door opened and the lilylike
lady with golden hair descended into the
water, and with gay laughter sported among
the waves.

"Again in the evening I saw her dancing
amid lights and gayety with the French count.

"Neither of them thought, nor had hearts
worthy to think of Emilie, to whom a life of
hardship and of sorrow had given riches of
which they had no power to conceive."

SCHEVENINGEN SHELL-GATHERER.

# AN ANCIENT FAMILY.

Truly the skill of the Great Architect of Nature is no less displayed in the construction of a sea urchin than in the building of a world.—EDWARD FORBES.

# XIII.

## AN ANCIENT FAMILY.

"Old Neptune's a spendrift! See the 'sand dollars he's thrown away! And here's a devil's pincushion! What does theology say about that?" asked Tom merrily.

"Theology and science take that spiny thing," answered the minister, " and read in its eventful history ' by what wonderful, what unexpected roads God arrives at the completion of his designs. One does not discern the slightest resemblance of form between the little slow-swimming dome (the infant sea urchin) and the spined and boxed urchin which crawls over the rocks.'

"So accustomed are we to the thoughts and to the skill of the Creator as manifested in his works, we are indifferent to the lessons they teach or to the prophecies they may contain. So much for your text, Tom!

"The sea urchin has several names besides the one which you bestowed upon it. Sea

porcupine it is called from the forest of spines
which cover its test. When dead these spines
rub off and the beautiful shell is apparent,
which then is not inappropriately called sea
egg. *Echinus* is the name science has given it.
This class of radiate animals belongs to the
group *Echinodermata*, which means spiny-
skinned, and truly the *Echinidæ* are a spiny
set. Yet those very spines are most wonderful examples of the divine handiwork. Their
tints are delicate and various; the substance
of which they are composed is a calcareous
matter, but transparent as glass. Each spine
is connected with the interior of the animal
and moved at its will. You have noticed the
tiny raised processes on the surface of a dead
urchin's shell; the spines have a depression
which exactly fits over this point in a manner similar to the ball-and-socket joints in the
human shoulder and hip.

"It is by help of these spines that the *Echinus* climbs even a smooth surface, or with
them excavates for itself a hiding place in the
sand. Many *Echini* are able by some means
to bore holes in rocks, and there spend their
days in seclusion and safety from enemies that
infest the sea.

"The mouth of the sea urchin is on the

A SEA LILY.

1. Pentacrinoid larva of the rosy feather star.
2. The bud quite young.
3. Dorsal view of the larva of the feather star at very early stage
   of its development, before the disappearance of the ciliated
   bands. Much enlarged.
4. Mature rosy feather star. (Comatula rosacea.)

under surface, and armed with five calcareous
teeth and strong muscular jaws it is well prepared to do its work of crushing small crustaceans and mollusks, which are its food.

"The starfish is the pretty cousin of the sea
urchin, and is a 'lineal descendant' of the 'old
family' *Crinoideæ*. There is, in fact, an *Asteria* who in its early life adheres to the time-
honored custom of its ancestry, and fixed to a
stalk attaches itself to some graceful seaweed
or aristocratic coralline. Their bodies, like
others of this group, are supported by calcareous envelopes composed of numerous pieces.
The number of these plates in the Red Sea
starfish, for example, is estimated to be eleven
thousand.

"Our starfish, as you know, has generally
five rays. *Solaster papposus* has ordinarily
thirteen ; another has more than thirty. In
one variety they are found many feet long.

"Some starfishes possess the power of growing another ray if one be broken off, and the
one sundered may grow four more and become starfish 'No. 2.' Not only this, but some
varieties are actually suicidal, flying to pieces
when taken from the water.

"The *Comatula rosacea*, or feathery star, is
one of the prettiest creatures you can imagine.

When young it grows upon a stem and waves in the sea as an aster—which it sometimes imitates in color as well as form—waves in the breezes. When it becomes fully developed it finds itself free from the restraining stem and floats out into the watery world at will or catches to stones, shells, and seaweeds by its feathery arms, holding with such tenacity that it would seem each bit of feather concealed a claw.

"You have heard how starfish delight in living upon mussel and oyster beds, being exceedingly destructive to the latter. If the oyster refuses to open its doors to Mr. Starfish, Mr. Starfish has a way of his own of opening them; and if the oyster still remains obdurate and refuses to be eaten, the starfish accommodates himself to circumstances and projects his stomach about the oyster and sucks in the soft parts. The stomach is capacious, extending its lobes into each arm or ray.

"Another relative of my lady fair—the stone lily—possessing her family traits but not always her charming attractiveness, is the *Holothurian* or sea cucumber. We do not observe in this unattractive specimen the delicate plates around insulated rounded cavities. Yet naturalists tell us the leathery exterior of the sea

FISHING FOR SEA CUCUMBERS IN THE PHILIPPINE ISLANDS.
HOLOTHURIDÆ.

cucumber is rudimentary calcareous matter arranged on the same plan as in the skeleton of its more attractive relatives.

"In color it is green, brown, or red, and its delicate tentacles are arranged over its surface, corresponding to the tiny points marking the vegetable which it so strongly resembles as to have received its name. In deep-sea dredgings specimens are often brought up about the size of a marketable cucumber.

"Although these strange creatures eat and drink they appear to attach very little importance to their stomachs, sometimes actually vomiting up their whole internal structure, and yet live on undisturbed ; in a few months the organs are reproduced.

"The sea cucumbers are found in many seas, but gain their greatest distinction on the coasts of China and Africa, where they are highly appreciated as articles of diet. In China they are prepared for market under the name of 'trepang.'

"Although upon first acquaintance these flowerlike animals do not appear to resemble each other, nevertheless we find they preserve the family characteristics of their distinguished progenitors, the stone lilies, so abundant in past ages that whole beds of marble have been formed almost entirely from their broken stems and flowers.

"Once the glory of the sea, they have dwindled to a few species, inhabiting for the most part the deepest seas."

The following may be helpful in giving an understanding of the classes of *Echinodermata*. First we have the *Crinoidea*, which are really stalked starfishes, the body mounted upon a stem which is jointed and hollow; second, the *Asteroidea*, which are free and have five arms; third, *Echinoidea*, having a spherical body, with long spines; fourth, the *Holothuroidæ*, having elongated bodies, with skin soft or muscular.

# BARNACLES.

There are castles by the sea ;
All their domes are porphyry.

Tell me who the builders be
Of these castles by the sea.

Anon.

116

## XIV.

### BARNACLES.

"Here we come to a pygmies' village," said Miss Bremely one day when the party were upon the beach. "I can scarcely step without shattering their tiny towers, they stand so thick upon the rocks."

"When the little tenants of these castles 'take the curl papers out of their hair,' and opening their two-valved doors look over their turrets, any small knight might be charmed into riding a tilt in their behalf," laughed the doctor.

"Don't barnacles live in these little castles?" questioned Undine.

"Yes," replied Dr. McLean; "though if you were to ask them who they were I fancy they would never know what to say. They have so many transitions I wonder if they know whether they are themselves or somebody else. In external appearance they resemble the mollusks; in more important parts of their organisms they are crustaceans.

"In their first form these little castle hold-
ers, but dancing atoms, have one big black eye,
three pairs of legs, and on the forehead a pair
of flexible horns. If we did not know the end
we should say a mistake had been made in
their legs, which seem to grow more and more
unfit for use either for land or water. 'Ascending the scale,' the body with its fringed
legs, to which are added two pair more, is now
inclosed in a tiny two-valved shell like a mussel. Its one eye becomes two, its head and
antennæ increase in size, and it now prepares
to make the most wonderful change of all. It
'stands on its head' literally and fastens itself
head downward to the rocks by means of a
cement itself secretes. Its bivalve shell is no
longer needed, its shield becomes the beginning
of its castle walls, and its group of legs become
tentacles which wave gracefully backward and
look like delicate curls of hair. It is these
which give the name *Cirripeda* to this group,
*cirrus* meaning a lock of hair and *pedes* a foot.

"They now are true barnacles, and their
castles by the sea are like turrets crowding one
upon another.

"All barnacles are not the same kind, and
their turrets are not all upon the rocks. Many
are attached to pieces of wood, hulls of ships,

BARNACLES.

Murex haustellum and Harpa imperialis, with attached barnacles.
Infant barnacles.

etc. Not infrequently vessels put into port and have these incrustations which grow burdensome, removed. Others, more nomadic perhaps in their dispositions, attach themselves to the bodies of whales, of sharks, etc., and while stationary are still among the greatest of travelers.

"When myths and science were much intermingled, the barnacle was believed to be the embryo of a goose, hence called the barnacle goose. We find one of the learned men of the sixteenth century describing: 'A thing in form like a lace of silke finely woven, the first that appeareth when the shell gapeth open. A little later the legs of the bird hang out. In short space of time it cometh to maturity and falleth into the water, where it becometh a fowl.' While science has dissolved this fable, it is known notwithstanding that the barnacle does pass through transitions quite as wonderful."

The children fell to examining barnacles, the doctor to musing, presumably upon science. Miss Bremely sat watching the waves that came riding up the sand like restless, foaming steeds. Presently she began singing softly Sidney Lanier's exquisite lines entitled

### BARNACLES.

My soul is sailing through the sea,
But the Past is heavy and hindereth me.
The Past hath crusted, cumbrous shells
That hold the flesh of cold sea-mells.
    About my soul
The huge waves wash, the high waves roll,
Each barnacle clingeth and worketh dole
    And hindereth me from sailing!

Old Past let go and drop i' the sea
Till fathomless waters cover thee!
For I am living, but thou art dead ;
Thou drawest back, I strive ahead
    The Day to find.
Thy shells unbind ! Night comes behind,
I need must hurry with the wind
    And trim me best for sailing.

The face of the singer was toward the sea,
and she did not know as she might if she had
looked into the doctor's eyes that he had ceased
to meditate upon science.

# A SEA FAN AND A SEA PARABLE.

What the cloud doeth
The Lord knoweth ;
The cloud knoweth not.
What the artist doeth
The Lord knoweth ;
Knoweth the artist not.-

SIDNEY LANIER.

Take therefore the talent from him—for unto every
one that hath shall be given ; but from him that hath not
shall be taken away even that which he hath.—*Bible.*

## XV

## A SEA FAN AND A SEA PARABLE.

Undine discovered a fan gorgon in the doctor's cabinet and begged to know what it was, while Tom was no less delighted with the varieties of coral the cabinet contained.

"Oh, that," said the doctor to Undine, "was a mermaid's fan, and no belle of *terra firma* could boast of a fan so gorgeous. Its tints were rose and yellow, green and lavender, and bedight with jeweled filigree it flashed until its glitter made a sort of daylight under the sea. It is called a fan gorgon, Undine, and when alive was even more dainty and charming in color, and far more glittering than I have described or can lead you to imagine. Dainty and beautiful enough it was to be called a mermaid's fan.

"It was long considered a singular and gorgeous sea plant, but the microscope has revealed it to be the home and the work of little polypi which naturalists had thought were

10

flowers. The polypier, or polypus stalk, of the sea fan, surrounded by only a semicalcareous crust, is flexible, the whole structure tough and elastic. Different species show various, but all beautiful formations. Sometimes the branches appear nearly straight, at others they are a mazy network of the most delicate and intricate tracery, and when their colonies of jewel-like polypi are in bloom they seem the realization of a fairy dream.

"*Gorgonidæ* are found in all seas, but are most abundant in those of warm climates, as is the case with all species of polypi.

"These fan manufacturers were cousins to the polypi who wrought those miracles in stone," continued the doctor, turning to Tom and the corals. "All these little workers have been known as *Zoöphytes*, or flower animals. They might have been called Philosopher's Puzzles, for such they have long been, and even now they keep many of their pretty secrets safe in their own little stomachs, this anatomical locality being at present regarded by the sages as the 'seat and center' of personal identity in these pretty polypi.

"In their living and active state each little worker looks like a tiny star with its rays arranged about the central point, which is the mouth.

"We are apt to regard such minute organisms as insensible to surrounding conditions, and unable to communicate with each other even if they might be conscious of anything to communicate, but we find Nature clothes her 'feeble folk' with mystery and endows them with faculties we can not understand; and if you were to injure or disturb one of the polyps in a piece of coral like this, quick as a flash would the danger be telegraphed to every member of the little colony, and you would see each tiny animal instantly curl back as if he had been the one who suffered.

"An enormous traffic is carried on in the different varieties of coral, affording employment for hundreds of vessels and thousands of fishermen. It is broken from the sea bottom by means of beams or irons attached to the boats used for that purpose, and brought up by grappling irons; divers also are employed in these coral fisheries. I once saw them in the Mediterranean gathering red coral (*Corallium rubrum*), the divers themselves looking like very unattractive mermen, or sea monsters, as they came up from the depths with the great

nets swung from their shoulders in which they
had deposited the coral.

"The bulk of coral used for ornamentation
is fished from the Mediterranean Sea, and sometimes at a depth of seven or eight hundred
feet.

"The red is susceptible of a fine polish, and
is much sought after by many Eastern nations
for personal adornment, for sword hilts, for
amulets, which are superstitiously believed to
have power to avert evil. The name given it
by the Greeks commemorated their belief that
it was originally the blood drops that fell
upon the seashore from the head of Medusa,
hardened and planted in the sea by ocean
nymphs.

"Formerly the red commanded the highest
price of all the corals, but this point has been
yielded to the delicate pink, which vies in
color with the tinted petals of the queen of
flowers.

"Besides the red, pink, and white coral,
there are many shades of green, brown, yellow,
and black. All are more or less beautiful, both
in life and in death.

"The flowerlike inhabitants have disap-
peared, but their workmanship remains in these
exquisite marbles before you, Tom," continued

the doctor in a more serious vein. "During their lives this dainty tracery was hidden, but now we can see the true beauty of the homes into which their lives were wrought. This calcareous substance secreted by these polypi is 'partitioned into cells with mathematical regularity, and, studding the entire surface, produces a most beautiful effect. The specific variety of these coral homes is almost endless, yet each species builds after its type. The lesson has been learned, and the creatures live up to it throughout endless generations.'"*

While Dr. McLean displayed the different varieties of coral which his cabinet contained, Miss Bremely said, "The quotation you have just given suggests to me a sea parable which I think contains a beautiful lesson." The doctor turned to her with a pleasant interest, and, interpreting his wish in the smile he gave, she repeated the following

---

* Henry A. Ward, in Catalogue of Corals, Gorgons, etc.

## SEA PARABLE.

"Beautiful coral," said a silvery wave, "I bring you chalk from yonder cliff; it will help you in your building!"

And the wave with the silvery crest sped on. "Hum!" exclaimed a crab, snapping at an annelid, "a stupid lot you corals are! You have no greater joy than to settle upon a rock and drudge your lives away in making buds little bigger than grains of sand. A pretty life to live! And you, Algæ, are no better," he growled, as with his "compound faceted eyes" he caught sight of seaweed upon the waves, "You spend your days spinning pink and purple laces! I am sick of seeing such drudgery."

And the crab backed into an empty shell upon the sand.

"Your life of leisure does not seem to have improved your disposition," said a receding wave, "You are fast losing the tal ents which were yours at the beginning. Have a care! I warn you!"

And the wave with the silvery crest sped on.

"It is true we are small and can do but little," whispered the Coral; "but the Master of Life created us for a glorious purpose. He has deigned to give us lovely visions, and has said to us in a voice sweeter than song, '*Build ye!*'"

"Yes," assented the *Corallium rubrum*) precious coral), "his presence suffused the clouds with a glow surpassing the beauty of the morning; fair tints commingled and veins of crimson and scarlet intertwined like delicate twigs. We are a feeble folk, and we knew not that we could be of any use, but a voice came out of the cloud, saying, '*Build* ye *on this wise!*' We knew not how, but in strong desire and overpowering love we dwelt upon the vision. Of ourselves we are no longer aware. We lose ourselves in obedience to the beautiful vision, and we feel an assurance that all is well."

A Wave touched lightly the pink and crimson *bijouterie* of the coral bed and whispered to the polypi: "In losing yourselves ye find honor and become the setting of crowns.

There is a crown whose jewels, like yours, are wrought in obedience and love, and of them it is said, 'They shall shine forever and ever!'" And the wave with the silvery crest sped on.

The *Tubipora musica* (organ-pipe coral) continued: "It was near the morning of creation; upon the sand stood One whom the earth and the sea adore, and at whose feet the white waves bow their heads. He gathered the hollow reeds that grew at his feet, and, pressing them together, he said to us: '*Build* YE *on this wise!*'

"We knew not how; yet the sea and all things that are therein praise him and do his will. We gave ourselves to the work, and behold! he hath blessed it, and that hath made it good."

A wave touched the tiny "organ pipes" of coral and a wind breathed upon them; a soft melody arose, in key with that harmony heard when the morning stars sang together. The wave with the silvery crest sped on.

"And to us," said one of the arborescent corals—the *Mandrepora formosa*—"the vision was given on this wise: The branching trees of the forest were reflected in the mirror of the ocean, and while in our feebleness we won-

A FAN GORGON.        HERMIT CRAB.

dered a power came upon us to build. We
gave ourselves; we could do no more. The
vision is ever before us. We would that we
could better accomplish the work that was
given us to do."

A wave circled among the branches of coral
and whispered to the little polypi: "I come
from laving a beautiful island where palm trees
grow and homes of mankind are clustering. It
was *you*, little 'reef builders,' who laid the
foundations of that island. Ye builded better
than ye knew." And the wave with the silvery crest sped on.

Upon the sand crawled a crab—he with the
"compound faceted eyes"! He of the race of
armored knights! But, alas! by generations
of indulgence and selfishness, lost was half his
coat-of-mail—which had been a family heir-
loom—two of his sets of claws, made strong
for service, had become enfeebled by disuse or
wholly followed the lost armor. He crawled
in terror upon the sand, seeking safety from
his legion of enemies. Spying the shell of an
industrious mollusk, he hastily devoured the
helpless creature and backed crabbedly into
its empty shell. The crab had become the
half-naked vagabond tramp of the seashore!

A wave broke upon the sand. It gave the

hermit crab a sad but disdainful toss, and said:
"I warned you long ago! This comes of not
doing your best with gifts the Creator bestowed
upon you!" And the wave with the silvery
crest sped on.

# A STORM.—RAZOR FISHES.

When winds are raging o'er the upper ocean,
  And billows wild contend with angry roar,
'Tis said, far down, beneath the wild commotion,
  That peaceful stillness reigneth evermore.

Far, far beneath, the noise of tempests dieth,
  And silver waves chime ever peacefully,
And no rude storm, how fierce soe'er it flieth,
  Disturbs the Sabbath of that deeper sea.

So to the heart that knows thy love, O Purest!
  There is a temple sacred evermore:
And all the babble of Life's angry voices
  Dies in hushed stillness at its peaceful door.

Far, far away the roar of passion dieth,
  And loving thoughts rise kind and peacefully,
And no rude storm, how fierce soe'er it flieth,
  Disturbs the soul that dwells, O Lord, in thee.

MRS. H. B. STOWE.

134

XVI.

A STORM.—RAZOR FISHES.—BYSSUS SPINNERS.
—STONE EATERS.—LIGHTED TOMBS.

In grandeur an approaching storm strode through the heavens, walked upon the waters, and thrilled the palpitating air.

Tom threw himself upon the ground under the very lashings of the ocean spray, but happy as a storm petrel he watched the marshaling of the tempest.

Dr. McLean stood with uncovered and up-lifted head. He felt the power and the presence of one mighty—

Who layeth the beams of his chambers in the waters :
Who maketh the clouds his chariot :
Who walketh upon the wings of the wind.

As the wind sweeps through a casement and smites an Æolian harp placed there by the builder, and of which till then the householder knew not, so were touched chords in this man's soul—chords placed there by the Master Build-er, to be used one day when the house should be

larger and the wind the "breath of the spirit."
He who in reverence and humility stood with
uncovered head was a quickened spirit. His
whole being thrilled with the consciousness of
these greater powers—of senses till then un-
recked of. Whether in the body or out of the
body, he knew his immortality—that he stood
before the face of the Eternal. He felt his
kinship.

A chill little hand was slipped into his.
He yearned for the fuller, further communion,
for the larger vision; but he turned from the
glory, from the vision, and bent to the child at
his side. He could only so be true to his kinship; and so the vision stayed in his soul.

Undine stood trembling; her pale face told
how the black storm clouds and the furious
sea terrified her.

"It all makes me feel so small and weak,"
she said; "as if the wind could carry me away
into the darkness and storm as it would carry
a leaf."

"Fudge!" exclaimed Tom, as he lay upon
his back, kicking his heels into the sand. "I
like it! It's grand! It makes me feel as if I
were an eagle and heard the swoop of eagles
overhead. My! don't the wind and the sea
roar!"

But Dr. McLean and his little charge were halfway to the cottage, she telling how troubled she felt for the dear people in ships out on that troughy sea, while he gently soothed her burdened little heart, leading her to rest her care on him who "ruleth the raging of the sea." He repeated the grand words of the Psalmist, whose inspiration touched all subjects and all ages:

> " They that go down to the sea in ships,
> That do business in great waters;
> These see the works of the Lord,
> And his wonders in the deep.
>
> .    .    .    .    .    .
>
> He maketh the storm a calm,
> So that the waves thereof are still."

They were none too soon in seeking shelter; just as they gained the veranda the vanguard of the storm struck them. Even Tom was constrained to leave his contemplation of "eagle wings" and make good use of a pair of stout legs. The shadows were gone from Undine's eyes, and they were full of merriment as she watched Tom dashing through the storm, sending back defiant peals of laughter to the gusts of wind and billows of rain that followed him.

The trio stood at the window watching the

waves and the rain "clap their hands together,"
as Tom expressed it.

"I should think such hammering waves
might break all the shells in the ocean," said
Undine, whose heart ever turned to her treasures.

"Many of them will be broken," answered
the doctor, "but not unfrequently some of the
most fragile are lifted upon the crest of a wave
and laid upon the sand, far out of danger;
some are buried in the sand. You know how
the limpets and abalones cling; more are down
in the region of calms below the storm, while
others are moored by stout cables of their own
spinning."

At mention of shells buried in the sand,
Tom pulled a razor shell from his pocket, saying: "When I was wading in the shallows
this morning a jet of water struck my foot. I
dug this fellow out of the sand."

"I once saw men searching for razor fishes
in the Bay of Naples," said the doctor. "They
were finding them with their feet, as you did
this one; but I venture you did not resort to
their method of bringing them to the surface.

"When they discover a *Solen*—another
name for their razor fish—they bring it up between their toes; and as the shell has a razor-

like edge, and the owner of it makes a fierce struggle for liberty, the poor fisherman often has his foot badly cut before the prize is secured.

"Razor fishes belong to the order *Siphoni-da*, some members of which are dubbed 'watering pots,' on account of their strong siphons, many inches in length. In fact, in the *Glycimeris generosa* of our own coast the siphon attains to a full yard.

"Their habit of spouting out jets of water when disturbed is one way by which they are discovered, and gives them the additional name of 'spoutfishes.'"

As the doctor finished, Undine asked: "What did you mean by saying, 'some shells were moored by cables of the animal's own spinning?'"

"Oh, those are the byssus spinners!" said the doctor, and going to a shelf he took several shells from it. First he displayed a pearly *Anomia*, the undervalve of which was flat, with a hole near one extremity to allow of the passage of the byssus tuft for attachment; then he showed them a scallop with a notch through which the stout byssus fiber was passed; then a mussel, saying: "The inmates of these shells knew how to spin a tuft of fibers which in

11

some were fine as silk, in others stiff and
horny. These were attached by strong muscles to themselves, and thence to rock, reef,
or wreck, as pleased the little spinner.

"These threads are spun by the foot of the
little animal, and are so stout as to withstand
the shock of the incoming seas. When wish-
ing temporary anchorage, or fearing the stress
of waves, it has only to throw out its byssus
cable and rest secure. Sometimes this little
bark with its silken moorings is freighted with
pearls," said he, pointing to a mussel; "the
pearls of these shells, however, are generally
of an inferior order.

"The *Pinna*, or fan mussel, is a byssus
spinner, having valves two feet long; and the
beautiful silk of its byssus has been used in
spinning rich and costly fabrics.

"We find among these not only the spinners of silk, but borers of wood and stone, and
hence some of them have received the name
'wood eaters' or 'stone eaters.'

"How these little creatures are able to bore
into hard substances has long been a question
of wonder and speculation. The serrated or
filelike edges of some shells might seem to
account for it in a measure; the abrading foot
with its strong muscles, sometimes assisted by

grains of sand which it rubs against the rock, might be sufficient; the cilia of others are said to be used in the boring. But none of these seem sufficiently to account for incisions made in flinty rocks or hardest of shell-like sub-stances. Hence it has been suggested that the work may be sometimes slowly but surely ac-complished by the means of an acid secreted by the bivalve for this purpose.

"Borers sometimes entirely bury themselves in rocky sepulchers of their own excavation.

"In tombs of men whom the world honors lights are sometimes kept burning. Nature honors equally these little miners, to whom she has given lamps while living; and after their busy days are over, their work done, and no man knoweth their sepulchers, still the light of their little lamps may be seen, for these borers are luminous; and it is said that the *Pholas* at least retains its phosphorescence so long as a piece remains; even if that piece be hard and dry it will again give out its light when moistened by the waves.

# OLIVES.

Ah! what pleasant visions haunt me,

   .       .       .       .       .       .

All the old romantic legends,
All my dreams come back to me.

LONGFELLOW.

Pages no better than blanks to common minds, to his are hieroglyphical of wisest secrets.—WILSON.

144

## XVII

## OLIVES.

" Why has no lover of Nature discovered the 'cipher' by which to read the hieroglyphics on these olives?" said Miss Bremely, after expressing her admiration for those glossy and finely polished shells.

"There is an exquisite pleasure in holding them in my hand and in hearing the rhythmic sound they make touching against each other. I have always been fond of them and always wished there might be such a thing as a clew to their pretty ' picture writing.'"

"Perhaps they are tablets of the Nereids, and report their calls, engagements, and conquests," suggested the doctor.

"Accept me as your oracle," he added, taking an *Oliva scripta* from her hand. "I will be a mouth to it. Its long-locked secrets shall speak to your heart.

"I affirm and declare this to be an ancient tablet from his Majesty Oceanus to her Royal

Highness Tethys, written in his fiery youth,
and full of titles of endearment. Behold this
one, oft repeated!" he said, pointing to certain
similar markings more delicately and regularly
traced than work on Babylonian brick or
Egyptian obelisk.

"Its reading is this: 'O maiden by my
heart cherished! The sea halls are desolate.
The jasper throne awaits thee. O maiden by
my heart cherished! The singing nymphs
can not charm me. Stay thy sliding chariot.
Listen and draw near. O maiden by my heart
cherished! Speaks not my heart to thee?'
And here," he said, "is inscribed the name
with all its titles and the ancient seal of the
great Oceanus."

While assuming to read the olive tablet the
doctor's eyes were really reading this later
maiden's face, and its blushes pleased him.

But she lightly answered:

"I read another story in this delicate cuneiform. It is an ocean rune full of mystery and
tells how the waves learned their motion; how
the moon draws the crystal tides; why the sea
moans; and this one has a sea song engraven
on it; and, presto!" she exclaimed, taking
from the shelf an elegant harp shell (*Harpa
ventricosa*), "here is the sea nymph's harp to

furnish the accompaniment. But I hear my
own little Sea-Maiden calling me."

And Miss Bremely was gone.

*Oliva scripta*, which the doctor had selected
as best illustrating his idea of an ancient tablet
or epistle from the royal Oceanus to his well-
beloved Queen Tethys, was delicate enough to
have been indeed a gift from a sea king to the
most lovely nymph either of the ocean or the
earth. This shell was over an inch in length,
shining as if polished by the jewel makers of
the deep. Its delicate fawn-colored surface,
suffused with soft shadings of brown, was written over in fine zigzag lines of a pale chestnut
tint, bearing also in stronger drawn hiero-
glyphic figures what seemed as if they might
be words or sentences to be emphasized; and
these oft repeated were the markings which
the doctor had ingeniously rendered into expressions of endearment, while just above the
aperture of the shell, which was a mingling of
the blue tint of the waves and the soft white-
ness of pearls, a strongly marked inscription he
affirmed to be the royal signature and seal.

The name given this Olive—*scripta*—
showed that others before had recognized in
its curious and delicate markings a resemblance
to writing.

Soft tints, a shining and porcellaneous surface, and handsome markings are some of the
characteristics of the shells of the family Olividæ. The animals of this family are exclusive-
ly tropical, and upon sandy flats of warm seas
they revel, moving about with considerable
quickness, burrowing under the wet sand when
the tides are low, and leaving no trace of their
hiding places.

The number of both fossil and living species is large, and it is impossible to tell all the
shades of coloring and the various patterns of
banding and nebulous painting to be found
upon them.

A curious characteristic of this group of
mollusks is its dual picturing. Underlying
the external porcellaneous and decorated surface of the shell is another layer decorated
with an entirely different pattern, the two layers making their different growths at the same
time. This under layer is, however, never exposed except by the outer one becoming worn
off or when acids are used in removing it.

The external colorings and markings of
these shells have also been obliterated by the
application of heat. So the Pacific islanders,
who delight in these shells for ornamenting
their bracelets and belts, but prefer them pure

white, have resorted to this trick in their extremely crude laboratories.

Another interesting peculiarity has been discovered in the olives in common with some other animals having similar shells, that is, the ability the little creature has of dissolving away the earlier formed volutions of the shell, and so according to its needs enlarging its place of habitation.

The islanders of the Indian Ocean fish the Olividæ extensively, using a number of lines baited with pieces of fish. They allow these lines thus baited to sink to the sandy shallows, the habitat of the olives. Not a very long time is required for the little animals to discover the feast thus spread for their use, and they gather upon the pieces of fish in great numbers, and are drawn up to be sold in the markets.

The Olivella, or little olive, is distinguished from the typical olive by a smaller shell, more extended spire, and the presence of a thin and horny operculum. It is also said that the olive has eyes while the Olivella has none.

The Indians of the Pacific coast attached a mercenary value to one variety of these small shells—*O. biplicata*—which they called "col-col."

There is another species which excels as a swimmer. Expanding quickly the lobes of its foot, it strikes the water suddenly with these and darts swiftly away in sportive fashion through the waves, or speeds at will from one sandy shoal to another.

Belonging to a subfamily of the Olividæ we find the harp shell, to which Miss Bremely referred as fitting to furnish the accompaniments to sea songs, which she fancied to be engraven upon the pretty olives. These harp shells are in truth beautiful enough to be suggestive of conceptions of harmony, of music, and of delight to sea nymphs and "ocean swells." The shells are prominently ribbed, and decorated with well-defined dark lines of intercostal painting. Most of them are highly colored, banded, and festooned in the richest manner. *Harpa ventricosa* and *Harpa articularis* are among the most beautiful.

Unlike some other beauties the Harpinæ all appear to delight in their large feet. So large are they in fact that their possessors are unable to accommodate them to their shells; so after the fashion of Cinderella's wicked sisters, who "would not need to walk when they were queens," they are said to detach a portion of the foot in emergencies.

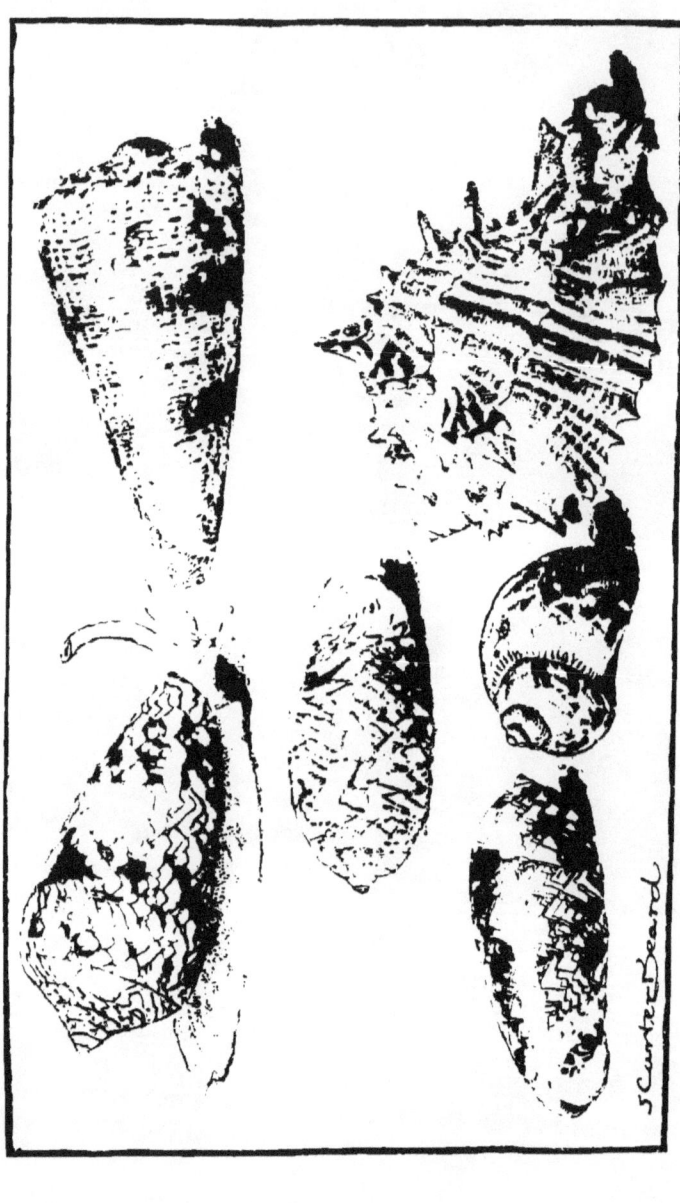

CONUS IMPERIALIS.

CONUS TEXTILE.

As if the spirit of beauty had taken possession of the *Harpinæ* and permeated them through and through, we find the animals themselves, as well as their shells, bright with bands and blotches of color.

There is a resemblance between some of the olives and the cone shells, as shown in our illustration; yet the differences in the living animals, as well as in the shells themselves, place them in distinct families. The *Olividæ* are destitute of an epidermis, which is one difference, as this characterizes the members of the *Conidæ*. Other distinctions mark them, yet each have the beautiful shining and pictured surfaces, as also has the *Phasianella*, the pretty pheasant shell of our engraving.

# GROWTH OF SHELLS.

Nature is man's best teacher. She unfolds
Her treasures to his search, unseals his eyes,
Illumes his mind, and purifies his heart;
An influence breathes from all the sights and sounds
Of her existence; she is Wisdom's self.

STREET.

But the cunning Little People,
The Puck-Wudjies knew the secret.

LONGFELLOW.

## GROWTH OF SHELLS.

"HERE's a pretty palace with a good stout front door," announced Tom, displaying a pearly *Trochus.*

"The name of that 'front door,'" said his cousin, "is the operculum. Many shells are furnished with opercula, but not all are so strong and horny as this. You see it is even thicker than the walls of the shell itself. It is developed upon a part of the foot of the animal and moved by strong muscles, which enable the little householder to shut his door quickly at the approach of an enemy.

"In the baby *Trochus* this operculum can be discerned, and grows with the growth of the animal and the other shell covering."

"I don't see how shells grow, anyway!" exclaimed Tom.

"Very likely you don't," said Miss Bremely. "Nature does not make a parade of her fine work, but if we care enough about her and

12          155

her mysteries to seek diligently for them she rewards us generously. You have learned that some shells secrete layers of *nacre*, with which many of our most beautiful ones are lined and which composes a great part of others. You remember, too, how injuries inflicted by borers are repaired. These facts open our eyes to a part of the mystery. Shells were once a portion of the mantle or delicate films which were separated from it. These gradually harden, becoming united to tissues previously thrown off by the mantle. So layer is joined to layer in forming shells so delicate a wave may break them or solid like these *Trochi*.

"Ridges, verices, and spines indicate some time has elapsed between the deposition of the layers.

"If shells are broken we can sometimes see the process of shell growth, if patient enough to watch the work and to wait the completion of the delicate repairing. First a moist exudation—a secretion from the injured part of the little animal—covers the spot. Gradually this exudation becomes filmy upon exposure to the air, and, as the process continues, grows calcareous or horny according to the character of the shell undergoing repairs.

"If the injury is sustained upon the walls

of a chamber which the animal has outgrown
and vacated, he does not again enter the 'halls
of the past,' but deliberately shuts out the past
and its injuries alike, by building a shelly wall
or partition entirely across that part of the
shell.

"The different depositions or layers are
sometimes shown when the edges of a shell become broken. They are also seen in the cameo
shells, in which the laminations are of different
colors. You will see what I mean by this,"
she said, unfastening from her collar a brooch
of shell cameo. Holding it to the light she
displayed the delicate translucence of the
orange ground over which figures were carved
from the next layer in white relief. "This
shows the strata of the shell," she said, "and
also how the colors have been turned to account
in carving the jewel. The shell from which this
was cut was known as *Cassis cornuta;* its habitat was the Indian Ocean.

"All cameos are not colored like this. Some
are a pale salmon on an orange ground. Such
are cut from the *Cassis rufa.* Others, from *C.
Madagascariensis* and *C. tuberosa,* have white
figures on dark claret-colored ground. Some
are cut from the *Strombus gigas*, which is the
pinky queen's couch of the West Indies. These

have raised figures of yellow on a pink ground.

"As has been seen, the shells used for these jewels and called cameo shells are generally the large *Cassides*. The carving of the cameos is a fine art, carried to an exquisite perfection by the Roman cameo cutters."

"What gives the different colors to shells?" asked Tom.

"That is another of the mysteries in which Nature has been chary of her confidences," answered Miss Bremely. "It seems to be in some way the result of a secreting work done by the border of the mantle. Light also is their painter. We observe that shells near the shore are richer and brighter in coloring than those which are shut out from the sunlight in deep ocean beds. Tropic seas yield us the most brilliantly colored shells, as tropic groves produce birds of gayest plumage.

"George W. Tryon tells us in his Conchology that 'bivalves which habitually lie upon one side have the upper valve colored and pictured, while the under valve is white and colorless.' He also quotes authorities who seem to have discovered in certain cases an adaptation in the color of shells to the color of objects upon which they rest.

"After all that has been said the mystery remains.  The delicate tracery upon the olives, the mottled surfaces of the *Cyprœa*, are mysteries still, and even *this* remains unaccounted for," she added, taking a *Nerita* from the shelf. "This tooth, like a point of ruby upon the columella, is a pretty secret which we can not explain.  This little jeweled point has given the name of 'bleeding tooth' to the shell.  We can not resist the wish that we might be near enough to Mother Nature's heart to be taken into her counsels.  We would like to know how and why she gave the little *Nerita* this single red jewel.  There are many things we would like to know."

# "THINGS UNRECK'D OF."

Great and gorgeous as is the display of Divine power and wisdom in the things that are seen of all, it may safely be affirmed that a far more extensive prospect of these glories lay unheeded and unknown till the optician's art revealed it. Like the work of some mighty genius of Oriental fable, the brazen tube is the key that unlocks a world of wonder and beauty before invisible, which one who has once gazed upon it can never forget, and never cease to admire.—PHILIP HENRY GOSSE.

There are more things in heaven and earth, Horatio,
Than are dreamt of in your philosophy.
                                    SHAKESPEARE.

"You have told us of little specks called eyes in some of our mollusca, but, Cousin Ellen, can these little animals really see and hear and do they ever speak to each other?" asked Undine.

"Some of them at least have organs of sight," answered Miss Bremely, "and eyes which have been considered rudimentary may simply be so because our own are not delicate enough to study them sufficiently.

"The eyes of the common snail are upon long stalks which are raised or lowered, turned this way and that as the animal travels, giving it quite the air of an interested observer. These eyes are very exposed upon their raised tentacles, and Nature has provided a very curious device for keeping them from injury— which is only another way of saying that the kind Creator has a care for even the eyes of a little snail. The point of these long stalks upon which the eyes are located can be drawn down through the tubes, as the finger of a glove is drawn in. The tubes are so trans-. parent one is able to see the black eye as it descends through the shortening tube to the little case under the skin of the head where it is safe.

"These little tentacles or eye stalks are so sensitive of danger that the least impression is telegraphed through the nervous organism of the animal, and in an instant the eyes are out of sight, and if danger still seems imminent, the cautious little creature glides quickly into his fortress.

"As proof of the clear vision of snails it is affirmed that they will go around obstacles in their path, and they appear to be attracted by bright colours.

"Among bivalves tiny specks have been detected near the borders of the mantle, some shining like jewels, others too small to be per- ceived except by a most careful scrutiny with a strong lens. These are supposed with good reason to be eyes. It has been observed that a sea urchin will sometimes turn its spines as if for self-defense in the direction in which a hand approaches to capture it.

"The razor fish, even when buried in the

sand with only the siphonal orifices exposed to the light, perceives the slightest shadow falling upon the water. This has led to closer study of the siphonal margins where what seem tiny eye specks have been detected.

"We are told that some of our shellfishes are supplied with auditorial nerves, while an external ear is credited to some. Yet their whole external surface is so extremely sensitive, aside from the especially sensitive tentacula, that they perceive the approach of any object by vibration; hence naturalists tell us we need not expect a very strongly developed sense of sound.

"Your last question I can best answer by reading you what some wise students have written concerning these interesting little creatures. 'If you ask what can be the use of ears to a class of animals which are invariably dumb, I answer though this is true with respect to the great majority, yet it may be only that our senses are too dull to perceive the delicate sounds which they utter, and which may be sufficiently audible to their more sensitive organs; and, besides, some mollusca can certainly emit sounds audible to us. Two very elegant species of sea-slug—viz., *Eolis punctata* and *Tritonia arborescens* (now called *Dendronotus arborescens*)—certainly produce audible sounds. Prof. Grant, who first observed the interesting fact in some specimens of the latter which he was keeping in an aquarium, says of the sounds, that they resemble very much the click of a steel wire on the side of the jar, one stroke only given at a time and repeated at intervals of a minute or two. . . . The sound is longest and oftenest repeated when the Tritoniæ are lively and move about, and is not heard when they are cold and without any motion. . . . The sound when in a glass vessel is mellow and distinct . . . and obviously proceeds from the mouth of the animal ; at the instant of stroke we observe the lips suddenly separate as if to allow the water to rush into a small vacuum formed within.'

"The following instance of affection among snails has been recorded by a naturalist who observed it : 'A pair of *Helix pomatia,* or Roman snails, were put in a garden for safe keeping. One of them escaped, but, finding its companion did not follow, it returned in quest of its fellow-prisoner.' "

# TROUBLE.

Life is full of ends, but every end is a new beginning, and we are constantly coming to the point where we may close one chapter, but we can always turn and open a new and better and diviner chapter.—PHILLIPS BROOKS.

## XX.

### TROUBLE.

"Cousin Ellen has a new ring," confided Undine to Tom soon after.

"That so?" responded Tom, in an uninterested voice.

"It's lovely," continued Undine; "a dear little diamond and some pearls."

"Don't see what she wants of any more rings!" ventured Tom, with more *esprit*. "She's more rings now than she can wear. I'd a thought she'd rather have a double-lens microscope, or an alligator—*I* would!"

Without appearing to notice Tom's preference, Undine gently touched the heart of the matter, and Tom's heart as well, by her next announcement: "I guess Dr. McLean gave it to her."

Tom's face grew troubled; he was silent a moment and then asked, "Undine, you don't s'pose Dr. McLean cares anything about Cousin Ellen, do you?"

"I don't see how he can help it, Tom; she's so lovely. Dr. McLean is nice, too," continued Undine; "the nicest man I ever saw—'cept papa," she added slowly.

"That's so," exclaimed Tom, "if he is a minister!"

"But, Tom, we can't spare Cousin Ellen," continued Undine, with dimming eyes.

"Course we can't!" agreed Tom. "Nor we can't spare the doctor either!" Evidently the children's problem was deepening.

At last Undine said with a sigh of mingled trouble and relief, "I'll talk with papa about it when he comes; he always helps us." And Tom, with hands deep in his pockets, went out whistling Three Blind Mice.

That evening with her head upon her father's broad shoulder, Undine sobbed out her story of the beautiful ring and the anxieties assailing her loving little heart.

Mr. Bremely laid his bearded face against her cheek and for several minutes was silent. His heart was far away with his own sweet, sad past. A tear upon his hand recalled him to the child to whom he must not only give strength and protection, but motherly comfort as well. Patting her cheek and smiling he agreed with her that "they could not spare

Cousin Ellen nor Dr. McLean—nor anybody," and promised he would look into the matter.

Undine's confidence in her father was only equaled by her love, and soon she was laughing gleefully while she searched his pockets for the strange money he told her he had brought her.

One pocket she found filled with cowries, yellow and shining. "Money cowries," her father told her they were called, because of their commercial value in some parts of Asia and Africa, to which places many tons weight have been carried annually by traders. "Orange cowries," said her father, "are the crown jewels of the Friendly Islanders, and are worn as marks of chieftainship. But go further, Undine; you will find other *Cyprœa* that will please your fancy." And truly the elegant "porcelain shells" she found in another pocket, with their exquisite enamel and beautiful mottling, called forth expressions of the greatest delight. Among the richly colored was a shell of purest white, all the fairer for its loneness. It was the *Ovulum ovum*, or "poached egg," as it is often called. Another very curious to her was the *Ovulum volva*, or "weavers' shuttle," as it is named, because of the prolongations of both ends of the shell.

13

From another pocket she brought out a handful of tiny points. "What are these?" she asked. "Are they ivory tusks of fairy elephants, or horns of baby unicorns?" And the rippling sound they made as they passed through her fingers pleased her ears as perhaps the "jingle" of these *Dentalian* "guineas" please the ear of the Indian money getter. The value of *Dentalia*, or "toothshells," she learned, was determined by the length of the shells.

Later that evening, when Undine and Tom had sailed away to the universe of dreams, Dr. McLean with Miss Bremely paused before the open door of the library. Mr. Bremely sat within, a book was open before him, but he could not read. His heart was stirred with a mighty past. An angel had come down that evening and troubled its waters.

The flush upon Miss Bremely's cheeks was again like the pink tint of shells, and dimples played among her blushes, while Dr. McLean looked as happy as a king; yet enigmatical as it seemed, they assured Mr. Bremely they came because they were in sore trouble. The doctor had learned, like Undine, that he could not spare Miss Bremely; and she that she could not spare Dr. Lean; and both, like the children, that they "could not spare anybody."

The consultation was long, but it was finally decided that Dr. McLean should leave his boarding house, and that the cottage among the acacia trees should for a time at least become the manse.

Mr. Bremely especially urged this, since business called him soon to South America for an absence of months.

Twice for the Bremelys, had the acacia trees lit their pale tapers of bloom. Ere they faded the second time, there was a wedding in the cottage and the acacia trees waved like palms with glory-lighted tops.

Trouble had passed. Dr. and Mrs. McLean walked in the heavenly peace of a true marriage.

Undine was serenely happy. Tom was jubilant. Mr. Bremely, with sad, glad eyes, blessed those whose love in turn was his blessing.

Among the gifts upon the occasion were two, for which the doctor was responsible, marked for the children: Undine found her package to contain the long-desired microscope, while Tom rejoiced over the coveted young alligator.

# INDEX.

Abalona, 64.
Acelephæ, 53.
Algæ, Chap. IX.
Ammonite, 86.
Anomia, 139.
Argonauta Argo, 83.
Argonaut, Chap. X.
Asteria, 111.
Avicula margaritifera, 61.
Awabi, 65.

Barnacles, Chap. XIV.
Borer, 20, 140, 141.
Byssus spinners, Chap. XVI.

Cassides, 165.
Cassis cornuta, 157.
Cassis rufa, 157.
Cassis madagascariensis, 157.
Cassis tuberosa, 157.
Cerripeda, 118.
Chitonidæ, 95.
Chiton Katherina, 95.
Chlorospermeæ, 75.
Comatula rosacea, 111.
Conidæ, 151.
Corallium rubrum, 125, 129.
Cornua Ammonis, 87.
Cowries, 171.
Crepidula, 51.
Crinoideæ, 111, 114.
Cyprœa, 171.

Dendronotus arborescens, 165.
Dentalia, 172.

Echinoidea, 114.
Echinodermata, Chap. XIII.
Echinus, Chap. XIII.

Feathery star, 111.
Fulgur canaliculatus, 18.
Fulgur carica, 18.

Glycimeris generosa, 139.
Gorgonidæ, 124.
Gorgon, Chap. XV.

Haliotis, 8, Chap. XVIII.
Haliotidæ, 64.
Harpa articularis, 150.
Harpa ventricosa, 146.
Helix pomatia, 166.
Hermit crab, Chap. XV.
Holothurian, 112, 113.
Holothuridæ, 114.
Hydroids, 45, 56, 57.

Ianthina fragilis, 37, 38.

Limpet, 5, 16, 17, 66.

Mactra solidissima, 94.
Malleus vulgaris, 64.
Mandrapora formosa, 130.

175

Medusæ, 47, 57, Chap. VII.
Melanospermeæ, 75.
Mermaid's cradle, 93, 97.
Mermaid's lace, 79.
Microscopic shells, Chap. IV.
Murex brandis, 28.
Murex palma-rosa, 29.
Murex princeps, 30.
Murex radix, 29.
Murex tinuispina, 29.
Murex tribulus, 29.
Murex trunculus, 28.
Murexes, Chap. III, 27.

Nautilus, 84, 86, Chap. XI.

Oliva biplicata, 149.
Oliva scripta, Chap. XVIII.
Olivella, 146.
Olives, Chap. XVIII.
Operculum, 154.
Ovulum ovum, 171.
Ovulum volva, 171.
Oyster, 8, Chap. VIII.

Patella, Chap. II.
Patella vulgatus, 22.
Pearls, Chap. VIII.
Pecten, Chap. II, 13, 14, 15.
Pecten Jacobæus, 22.
Phalos, 141.
Phasianella, 151.
Physalia, 54.
Pinna, 140.
Pinna noblis, 64.
Portuguese man-of-war, Chap. VII.
Purpuras, Chap. III.

Razor fishes, 22, Chap. XVI, 164.
Rhodospermeæ, 75.

Salpæ, 45.
Sand dollar, Chap. XIII.
Sapphirina ovatolanceolata, 45.
Sargasso Sea, 76.
Sargassum bacciferum, 76.
Scalaria, 45.
Scallop, Chap. II, 13, 14, 15.
Scheveningen shells, Chap. XII.
Sea fan, Chap. XV.
Sea slugs, 165.
Sea snails, 22.
Sea urchin, Chap. XIII.
Serpula, 22.
Siphonida, 139.
Solaster popposus, 111.
Solen, 138.
Snails, 163, 164.
Starfish, 8, Chap. XIII.
Strombus gigas, 157.

Tradaena gigas, 95.
Triton tritonis, 40.
Triton variegatus, 40.
Tritonia, 39.
Tritonia arborescens, 165.
Tritoniæ, 166.
Trochus, 155.
Tubipora musica, 130.

Unio Hyria, 63.

Venus Californiensis, 94.
Venus mercenaria, 94.

Worm cases, 45.

THE END

## APPLETONS' HOME-READING BOOKS.

### Edited by W. T. HARRIS, A. M., LL D.,

*U. S. Commissioner of Education.*

A comprehensive series of books presenting upon a symmetrical plan the best available literature in the various fields of human learning, selected with a view to the needs of students of all grades in supplementing their school studies and for home reading. It is believed that this project will fully solve the long standing problem as to what kind of reading shall be furnished to the young, and what will most benefit them intellectually as well as morally.

*NOW READY.*

*THE STORY OF THE BIRDS.* By JAMES NEW-TON BASKETT. 65 cents *net.*

"Mr. Baskett's book is not to be easily disposed of in a few words; it is out of the common run of popular ornithology, and decidedly original We attest the author's competence for clear statement of facts, and the thorough readability of his whole book."
—*The Nation.*

*THE PLANT WORLD : Its Romances and Realities.* Compiled and edited by FRANK VINCENT, M. A., author of "Actual Africa," etc. 60 cents *net.*

"Its interest will extend to every member of the family, to every one who loves Nature, for its information regarding the plant world will make the mysteries of springtime the more significant, the more beautiful."—*Boston Times.*

*THE STORY OF OLIVER TWIST.* By CHARLES DICKENS. Condensed for home and school reading by ELLA BOYCE KIRK. 60 cents *net.*

"The language is unchanged, expressions are not modified, but everything a child would be likely to skip has been elided. The action is thus accelerated to suit the most impatient reader."—*Chicago Evening Post.*

*IN BROOK AND BAYOU; or, Life in the Still Waters.* By CLARA KERN BAYLISS. 60 cents *net.*

In this volume the author introduces her readers to some of the interesting inhabitants of the microscopic world by the aid of numerous plates and full descriptive text. The account of the evolution of these minute creatures and their struggle for existence is given in a remarkably entertaining way, and makes the book as fascinating as a novel.

*IN PRESS.*

*CURIOUS HOMES AND THEIR TENANTS.* By JAMES CARTER BEARD.
*CRUSOE'S ISLAND.* By F. A. OBER.
*UNCLE SAM'S SECRETS.* By O. P. AUSTIN.
*NATURAL HISTORY READERS*, 5 vols. By J. F. TROEGER.
*THE HALL OF SHELLS.* By Mrs. A. S. HARDY.

*(Others in preparation.)*

# D. APPLETON & CO.'S PUBLICATIONS.

## THE LIBRARY OF USEFUL STORIES.

*Each book complete in itself. By writers of authority in their various spheres. 16mo. Cloth, 40 cents per volume.*

**NOW READY.**

*THE STORY OF THE STARS.* By G. F. CHAM-BERS, F. R. A. S., author of "Handbook of Descriptive and Practical Astronomy," etc. With 24 Illustrations.

"The author presents his wonderful and at times bewildering facts in a bright and cheery spirit that makes the book doubly attractive."—*Boston Home Journal.*

*THE STORY OF "PRIMITIVE" MAN.* By EDWARD CLODD, author of "The Story of Creation," etc.

"No candid person will deny that Mr. Clodd has come as near as any one at this time is likely to come to an authentic exposition of all the information hitherto gained regarding the earlier stages in the evolution of mankind."—*New York Sun.*

*THE STORY OF THE PLANTS.* By GRANT ALLEN, author of "Flowers and their Pedigrees," etc.

"As fascinating in style as a first-class story of fiction, and is a simple and clear exposition of plant life."—*Boston Home Journal.*

*THE STORY OF THE EARTH.* By H. G. SEELEY, F. R. S., Professor of Geography in King's College, London. With Illustrations.

"It is doubtful if the fascinating story of the planet on which we live has been previously told so clearly and at the same time so comprehensively."—*Boston Advertiser.*

*THE STORY OF THE SOLAR SYSTEM.* By G. F. CHAMBERS, F. R. A. S.

"Any intelligent reader can get clear ideas of the movements of the worlds about us. . . . Will impart a wise knowledge of astronomical wonders."—*Chicago Inter-Ocean.*

*THE STORY OF A PIECE OF COAL.* By E. A. MARTIN, F. G. S.

"The value and importance of this volume are out of all proportion to its size and outward appearance."—*Chicago Record.*

*THE STORY OF ELECTRICITY.* By JOHN MUNRO, C. E.

"The book is an excellent one, crammed full of facts, and deserves a place not alone on the desk of the student, but on the workbench of the practical electrician."—*New York Times.*

*THE STORY OF EXTINCT CIVILIZATIONS OF THE EAST.* By ROBERT ANDERSON, M. A., F. A. S., author of "Early England," "The Stuart Period," etc.

New York · D. APPLETON & CO., 72 Fifth Avenue.

# FAMILIAR FLOWERS OF FIELD AND GARDEN. By F. Schuyler Mathews.

Illustrated with 200 Drawings by the Author, and containing an elaborate Index showing at a glance the botanical and popular names, family, color, locality, environment, and time of bloom of several hundred flowers. 12mo. Library Edition, cloth, $1.75 ; Pocket Edition, flexible covers, $2.25.

In this convenient and useful volume the flowers which one finds in the fields are identified, illustrated, and described in familiar language. Their connection with garden flowers is made clear. Particular attention is drawn to the beautiful ones which have come under cultivation, and, as the title indicates, the book furnishes a ready guide to a knowledge of wild and cultivated flowers alike.

"I have examined Mr. Mathews's little book upon 'Familiar Flowers of Field and Garden,' and I have pleasure in commending the accuracy and beauty of the drawings and the freshness of the text. We have long needed some botany from the hand of an artist, who sees form and color without the formality of the scientist. The book deserves a reputation."—*L. H. Bailey, Professor of Horticulture, Cornell University.*

"I am much pleased with your 'Familiar Flowers of Field and Garden.' It is a useful and handsomely prepared handbook, and the elaborate index is an especially valuable part of it. Taken in connection with the many careful drawings, it would seem as though your little volume thoroughly covers its subject."—*Louis Prang.*

"The author describes in a most interesting and charming manner many familiar wild and cultivated plants, enlivening his remarks by crisp epigrams, and rendering identification of the subjects described simple by means of some two hundred drawings from Nature, made by his own pen. . . . The book will do much to more fully acquaint the reader with those plants of field and garden treated upon with which he may be but partly familiar, and go a long way toward correcting many popular errors existing in the matter of colors of their flowers, a subject to which Mr. Mathews has devoted much attention, and on which he is now a recognized authority in the trade."—*New York Florists' Exchange.*

"A book of much value and interest, admirably arranged for the student and the lover of flowers. . . . The text is full of compact information, well selected and interestingly presented. . . . It seems to us to be a most attractive handbook of its kind."—*New York Sun.*

"A delightful book and very useful. Its language is plain and familiar, and the illustrations are dainty works of art. It is just the book for those who want to be familiar with the well-known flowers, those that grow in the cultivated gardens as well as those that blossom in the fields."—*Newark Daily Advertiser.*

"Seasonable and valuable. The young botanist and the lover of flowers, who have only studied from Nature, will be greatly aided by this work."—*Pittsburg Post.*

"Charmingly written, and to any one who loves the flowers—and who does not?—will prove no less fascinating than instructive. It will open up in the garden and the fields a new world full of curiosity and delight, and invest them with a new interest in his sight."—*Christian Work.*

"One need not be deeply read in floral lore to be interested in what Mr. Mathews has written, and the more proficient one is therein the greater his satisfaction is likely to be."—*New York Mail and Express.*

"Mr. F. Schuyler Mathews's careful description and graceful drawings of our 'Familiar Flowers of Field and Garden' are fitted to make them familiar even to those who have not before made their acquaintance."—*New York Evening Post.*

New York: D. APPLETON & CO., 72 Fifth Avenue.

*B*IRD-LIFE. *A Guide to the Study of our Common Birds.* By FRANK M. CHAPMAN, Assistant Curator of Mammalogy and Ornithology, American Museum of Natural History; Author of " Handbook of Birds of Eastern North America." With 75 full-page Plates and numerous Text Drawings by Ernest Seton Thompson. 12mo. Cloth, $1.75.

" ' Bird-Life ' is different from other books. It deals with birds that are familiar, or half familiar; it interests the ignorant reader at once, and it makes the relations between birds and men seem more intimate. The economic value of birds will be better appreciated after reading this book."—*Boston Herald.*

" Contains more information about birds, in the same space, attractively as well as concisely stated, than can be found in any other book with which we are acquainted. . . . A delightful, valuable, instuctive, entertaining, beautiful book."—*Brooklyn Standard-Union.*

" Most heartily can ' Bird-Life' be commended. It is by a practical ornithologist, but it is simple and comprehensible. It is compact, pointed, clear. . . . The work is perfectly reliable. . . . The author uses every line to give information. A straightforward and very compact guide-book to bird-land."—*Hartford Post.*

" An intelligent consideration of the book will add to the reader's pleasure in his walks in field and wood, quicken his ear, make him hear and see things which before went unnoticed. . . . Gives the student an introduction to ornithology, which places him on the threshold of the entrance to the innermost circles of bird-life."—*Boston Times.*

" Mr. Chapman's book ought to be as greatly in demand in the average household as a history of one's country."—*Providence Journal.*

" The illustrations are undoubtedly the best bird drawings ever produced in America."—*Recreation.*

" A comprehensive book, one that is sufficient for all the ordinary needs of the amateur ornithologist. It is satisfactory in every detail, and arranged with a care and method that will draw praise from the highest sources. Every lover of outdoor life will find this book a delightful companion and an invaluable aid."—*Buffalo Enquirer.*

" A volume exceptionally well adapted to the requirements of people who wish to study common birds in the simplest and most profitable manner possible. . . . As a readily intelligible and authoritative guide this manual has qualities that will commend it at once to the attention of the discerning student."—*Boston Beacon.*

" Such a study as every intelligent reader will desire to make, even the busiest of them. . . . The author is in every way fitted for the task he has taken, and his book abounds in its facts of value, and they are pleasingly and gracefully told."—*Chicago Inter-Ocean.*

" An interesting mass of data collected through years of study and observation. . . . While accurate from a scientific point of view, it makes delightful reading for those who will soon be among the flowers and the fields."—*Philadelphia Inquirer.*

*INSECT LIFE.* By JOHN HENRY COMSTOCK, Professor of Entomology in Cornell University. With Illustrations by ANNA BOTSFORD COMSTOCK, member of the Society of American Wood Engravers. 12mo. Cloth, $2.50.

"A capital book for students, as well as a handbook for teachers, amateurs, and those interested in Nature. . . . Any one who will go through the work with fidelity will be rewarded by a knowledge of insect life which will be of pleasure and of benefit to him at all seasons, and will give an increased charm to the days or weeks spent each summer outside of the great cities. It is the best book of its class which has yet appeared."—*New York Mail and Express.*

"For class use no better book could be devised. But the amateur and summer tourist will find it equally valuable, because it opens up realms of investigation and delight that are infinite in their extent and variety. . . . A work that must take first place in the class to which it belongs."—*Philadelphia Press.*

"So easy has the author made the gaining of knowledge concerning insect life that even adults who perhaps have never given the subject a thought are very likely, if they take up the book, to become at once fascinated."—*Boston Globe.*

"It is just the book for those who on their vacations wander among the ponds and brooks, dandelions and locusts, long-horned beetles and roadside butterflies, and who live in the isles and the forests for several weeks to come. . . . The book must take first rank among works of its kind."—*New York Commercial Advertiser.*

"The volume is admirably written, and the simple and lucid style is a constant delight. . . . Is sure to serve an excellent purpose in the direction of popular culture, and the love of natural science which it will develop in youthful minds can hardly fail to bear rich fruit."—*Boston Beacon.*

"A more agreeable introduction to the study of the ways of the tiny winged things of the air and their metamorphoses in earth and water could not well be devised."—*Detroit Free Press.*

"A book like this is a good thing to put in the hands of young folks to make them see what is outside of their little home and school world, and to teach respect for other forms of life."—*Brooklyn Eagle.*

"The book teaches something on every page, yet on every page the student is told to go to Nature, to search out and observe for himself. Nor is it the young only who may find pleasure and profit in the use of this book. . . . The whole scheme and execution of 'Insect Life' are admirable."—*Buffalo Express.*

"To teachers, students, and the general reader who is fond of Nature, the book will commend itself, for it easily surpasses any volume in its field."—*San Francisco Chronicle.*

"A very practical book, and one that anticipates every need of the amateur in starting upon the study of insects. . . . Particularly desirable for summer vacation among the fields and woods. . . . Prof. Comstock's book fills a real want."—*New York Times.*